# A Girl Named Summer

## Julie Garwood

SCHOLASTIC INC.
New York Toronto London Auckland Sydney

ISBN 0-590-33770-X

12 11 10 9 8 7 6 5 4 3         0 1 2 3 4/9

For G.R., Elizabeth, Bryan and Gerry,
with love.

# A Girl Named Summer

A Wildfire® Book

# One

"Mother, does Michael have to wear that towel *all* the time?" Summer Matthews muttered. She knelt down in front of her three-year-old brother and looked him squarely in the eye while she snapped the oversized safety pin in position just below his chin.

"I can't be Superman without my cape," Michael replied. He frowned until the spray of freckles across the bridge of his nose became one brown streak. "Everyone knows you gots to wear a cape if you're going to be Superman," he continued in a tone of voice that suggested his older sister was definitely simpleminded.

"Of course you do, dear, and it's 'have to wear,' not 'gots to wear,'" their mother answered. Summer glanced up and watched her mother hunt through her gigantic purse. She's lost her keys again, Summer thought in exasperation.

"Mother, at least make him take off those ridiculous boots while he's in the house," she pleaded. She turned back to her brother and flipped the bright red towel back over his small shoulders. "Michael, fur-lined boots are terrific when you want to play in the snow, but it just happens to be the beginning of June."

From the belligerent expression on Michael's face, Summer concluded that her cool logic wasn't making a dent, so she tried another approach. "Your feet are going to get all shriveled up and fall off if you don't let some air get to them," she warned in an ominous voice.

Michael didn't bat an eye over that threat, Summer noticed. But then, her little brother wasn't easily intimidated. "Superman always wears red boots," he proclaimed. He rolled his eyes heavenward, just like Grandfather did when he was exasperated, and folded his arms in a militant manner across his chest. He was obviously in one of his stubborn moods, Summer finally realized, and she sighed with defeat.

"Summer, don't tease your brother," their mother admonished as she continued to pull items out of her purse.

"I give up," Summer said. "Your keys are on the dining room table," she added as an afterthought. "I just remembered seeing them there."

"Why, of course they are," her mother

exclaimed with a grin. "Michael, you be a good boy and obey your sister while she's in charge. Summer, don't forget to give your grandfather his medicine at three o'clock. It's on top of the refrigerator."

"Tell her I get to wear my boots," Michael demanded.

"Of course you must wear your boots," their mother agreed. "But please take them off during naptime."

"You win, half-pint," Summer said. She watched her mother kiss and hug Michael, and stood up to allow her mother to kiss her on the cheek.

As soon as her mother left, Summer turned to her brother. "Come on, I'll fix your lunch."

"No." It was an automatic response, a word Michael had grown quite fond of lately. Summer didn't pay any attention and walked into the kitchen. Michael followed her, hovering in the doorway while he watched her fix his sandwich.

"I'm not hungry," he stated in his stubborn voice when she placed the sandwich on the table.

"Yes, you are," Summer answered. She scooped him up and settled him in his chair before he could continue his rebellion, and sat down opposite him.

"I won't eat."

Summer pretended a bored yawn and shrugged. She had learned the hard way to act like she could care less when she really wanted something from Michael. One had to be an amateur psychologist when dealing with three-year-olds.

"Quit making squishes in your sandwich," she scolded him.

Michael looked at Summer. "Why are you so mad?" he asked.

"Mad? I'm not mad, Michael. Why should I be mad? My entire summer vacation is completely totaled, but that shouldn't make me mad, now should it?"

Wide, blue eyes stared at her; they were replicas of her own. Although they looked very much like sister and brother, Michael's hair was the color of the carrot slice he was now stabbing his sandwich with, while Summer's hair was a deep auburn tone. "Quit staring at me and eat."

Summer was in a rotten mood. "Life is the pits, Michael. Regina finally got her dad to let us work at the Pizza Paddle he owns, and now I have to stay home with you and Grandpa!"

Why am I sitting here trying to discuss my problems with a three-year-old? Summer suddenly asked herself. Good heavens, she was getting as strange as the rest of her family! And they were strange. Summer had come to that realization years ago, even before Grandfather had moved in with them. Her grandfather spent almost every waking hour down in the basement working on his inventions, so he fit right into her eccentric family.

"Anybody home?" The high-pitched voice of Regina Muntz, Summer's best friend, brought a smile to Summer's face.

"Come in," Summer yelled. "We're in the kitchen."

Regina bounded into the room but didn't stop until she was hunting through the refrigerator. "Hungry?" Summer teased. It was a joke, of course. Regina was always hungry.

Regina shrugged a reply. She crossed over to the kitchen table with an apple in her hand and a can of grape soda in the other and plopped down with all the grace of a skinny giraffe. "Hi, Mike. Summer, I just got back from my checkup at the doctor's, and I grew another inch," Regina mumbled between bites of apple. "I'm going to be an amazon, I just know it."

"No, you're not," Summer said with heartfelt sympathy. She knew how awkward Regina felt about her height and wanted to help her feel better. After all, they were best friends. "When the boys catch up with you — "

"Summer, I measured five feet, seven and a half inches," Regina snapped. She visibly winced with the admission. "Maybe I should try out for the boys' basketball team," she added in a calmer voice.

"Don't be silly. You'd kill yourself. There isn't a coordinated bone in your body," Summer replied with complete honesty. She knew she wasn't hurting Regina's feelings. They were too close. Besides, it was the truth. "Anyway, you're going to be a model, remember? And it's good for models to be tall and thin, and . . ."

". . . flat-chested," Regina supplied, "which I most definitely am. Let's change the subject. This is depressing. Where is everyone? It's actually quiet."

"Mom's working at the flower shop with Dad, and Grandpa is . . ."

". . . in the basement," Regina supplied. She had the habit of finishing Summer's sentences for her and sometimes that trait bothered Summer, but not today. "Has he finished his remote-control vacuum cleaner?"

Regina understood about Grandpa. And she never laughed. That's one of the reasons she's my best friend, Summer acknowledged. She *really* understood.

"I think so, but he hasn't tried it out upstairs yet. He's working on car chains today."

Regina nodded and they both smiled at each other. Yes, Regina definitely understood Summer's family.

"Can I play with Andy?" Michael interrupted with a loud, proud burp.

Usually Michael went right down for his nap after lunch, but Summer wanted to visit with Regina before hassling with her brother. "For a little while, *if* you finish your sandwich," she started to answer, but he was already running out the back door.

Summer turned to her friend. "There's no

easy way to tell you this, Regina," Summer said. "Mom has to work with Dad all summer. Mrs. Nelson is going to have a baby and she took the whole three months off."

"You're kidding! What about working at the Pizza Paddle?"

"I can't," Summer mumbled.

"Summer, do you realize how much time and effort went into my nagging Dad until he agreed to let us work there?"

Summer sat in dejected silence while she considered her bleak future. There wasn't any hope, she decided. What other fifteen-year-old girl stayed home all summer? Probably none. And this was the summer she and Regina vowed that they would make some new friends and meet some fantastic older boys. They had both agreed to turn over a new leaf, too, starting with their looks. Summer had decided that her clothes were entirely too juvenile, for one thing. The money she was going to make at the Pizza Paddle would enable her to buy some really fantastic outfits. Well, that was definitely out now. Mom and Dad couldn't afford to pay her more than a few dollars a week for baby-sitting. It would take her most of the summer just to have enough to buy a new skirt!

"You're going to be stuck here all summer?" Regina's voice made it sound like Summer had been sentenced to Siberia. Of course, taking care of Michael and her grandfather was probably just as bad, Summer thought, then immediately felt guilty.

"But what about our plans?" Regina's stubborn streak was asserting itself. She was just as disappointed as Summer was, and that fact made Summer feel somewhat better. "You'll never meet anyone if you don't get out there and circulate. That's what is so super about working at the Pizza Paddle. Everyone goes there on Friday nights. You know that!"

"I know, I know," Summer said. "But there isn't anything I can do about it. I tried to talk to Dad, but when he started his 'A Family Is A Team' lecture, I knew it was a lost cause."

"Ann Logan is having a swim party next week," Regina said, changing the subject.

"Oh, how splendid." Summer's voice reeked with sarcasm. *Splendid* was one of Ann's favorite words, and Ann was one of Summer's *least* favorite persons.

"Your claws are showing," Regina said with a giggle. "Just because she stole Eric from you. . . ."

"Don't start," Summer demanded. "And she did not steal him from me. I never had him to begin with, remember? That was all in your mind."

Ann Logan was definitely a thorn in Summer's side. As soon as she found out Summer was interested in Eric, she had moved right in. Eric was helpless before Ann's practiced assault. He never stood a chance.

"Do you think she uses lemon juice on her

hair? It's getting more and more streaked, I noticed."

"Who cares? She still looks like a Barbie doll with that plastic smile of hers. And the way she bats those lashes you'd think she had a tic or something."

"Well, she has to be nice to me," Regina said. "She still hasn't given up on Gregg."

"How can your brother stand her? Honestly, Michael has a better vocabulary than she does, and she acts so . . . phoney. I don't think she can hold a serious thought for more than ten seconds." The disgust was obvious in Summer's voice.

"Oh, all the boys like to have girls gush over them. That's our problem, Summer. We just aren't gushy enough. Anyway, I was invited to the party because of Gregg, that's for sure. We both know she really doesn't like me. She doesn't like any girl for that matter. Maybe I won't go, if you're not invited."

"You have to go. This will be the perfect opportunity for you to meet some new boys. With Ann's reputation to maintain, I'm sure there will be an abundance of . . ."

". . . gorgeous males surrounding her," Regina said. "We're supposed to bring dates," Regina added. "I guess I could ask Carl Benson. He's tall enough. If only he didn't tend to lisp. . . ."

"He does not lisp," Summer said and then promptly giggled. "And if he does, it's because of his braces. Besides, once you get there, you can . . ."

". . . circulate," Regina finished for her. "You're right. I'll ask Carl. I wish you were going though. I — wait! I've got it! You can go with Gregg."

"Oh, I don't know —"

"He'll do it," Regina interrupted, a glint of steel entering her brown eyes. "He owes me, Summer. I'll tell him tonight."

"Let me think about it first," Summer stalled.

"Look, we both said we would take advantage of every opportunity if we were going to change our images. Hermits don't meet many new people. Think about that."

"Okay, okay."

"I have to go. I'll call you later."

"Fine," Summer replied. She followed Regina to the front door, dodging toy cars and trucks along the way. It would take her most of the afternoon to clean up Michael's mess. And he had made the clutter in less than ten minutes.

"Want to do something tonight?" Regina asked.

"Can't. It's bingo night."

"Poor Summer. . . . Maybe your grandfather won't want to go tonight."

When it snows in July, Summer thought. "No chance. And don't say 'Poor Summer,'" she demanded. "I feel bad enough as it is."

"Summer honey, I'm talking to you," her

father said at the dinner table that night.

"Sorry, Dad. I guess I was daydreaming," Summer lied.

"Couldn't have been a good daydream, girl. You're frowning yourself into an early set of wrinkles," her grandfather bellowed from across the table. Since Grandfather had a bit of a hearing problem, he assumed everyone else did, too.

"I signed Michael up for swim lessons," her father said. "He starts tomorrow. He's to be at the park by ten, honey."

"Okay, Dad. How long are the lessons?" Summer asked, trying to force some enthusiasm into her voice.

"A half hour each morning for two weeks, except Saturdays and Sundays, of course."

"What about Grandfather?"

"I can manage on my own, girl," her grandfather answered. "Now hurry up and finish your dinner. I won't stand for being late for bingo."

It was a ritual. Every Monday night, regardless of the weather, Summer dutifully walked with her grandfather to the church hall two blocks away. While he played bingo, Summer helped Mr. Clancy at the snack bar.

If the truth were known, Summer really looked forward to bingo night, though she would die before admitting that fact to anyone, even Regina. The reason was her grandfather. He seemed to come alive on Monday nights, and it meant a lot to Summer to help him enjoy himself so much.

Summer gave a salute and hurried to fetch her purse. She then stood patiently at the front door for a good ten minutes while her grandfather gathered up the tools of his trade: a green ink dobber, scotch tape, and, of course, an extra pair of glasses in the event of an emergency. Grandfather took bingo seriously.

He was finally ready. Summer linked her arm through his and slowly began to walk. It was a lovely night, warm and breezy, the air alive with a multitude of scents of budding flowers.

"Do you like living with us, Grandfather?" Summer asked.

"Never a dull minute," her grandfather answered with a chuckle. "More like living in a zoo with all the commotion going on. Still, it's much better than that nursing home your daddy rescued me from."

"But you were the one who insisted on going there," Summer protested. "Dad says you just wanted to give up after Grandmother died. I'm glad you didn't like it there," she confessed. "And that you moved in with us. It's where you belong." Her grandfather smiled at her; there was a special bond between them. Summer could confide things to her grandfather. He never seemed bored with her chatter, even though he would occasionally fall asleep in the middle of a sentence. It wasn't from boredom, he always assured Summer. He just needed his rest.

"You still moping because you didn't get to go to Michigan with that rich girl friend of yours?" her grandfather asked bluntly.

"Grandpa, I wasn't . . . well, I *was* moping, but not anymore," she admitted with a sheepish grin. "And Mary Lou isn't the rich girl friend. You're thinking of Regina."

"Regina, the big girl with the pool in her backyard?" her grandfather asked. At Summer's nod, he continued. "She's a nice girl, even if she isn't Irish."

Summer laughed and shook her head. It was a fact that her grandfather set great store in his heritage.

"It would be nice to be Irish *and* rich, don't you agree?" she asked.

"You are rich, girl. You're healthy and belong to a caring family. What more could you ask for?"

Summer didn't have time to answer. They had reached the entrance to the church. Her grandfather threw his shoulders back and marched with a dignified stride toward the bingo cards. Summer waited until he had selected his cards and then helped him get settled in his spot, right next to John Abrams.

There was a crowd in front of the snack bar and Summer hurried to help Mr. Clancy. Only when she had rounded the corner to enter the snack bar by the side door did she realize that Mr. Clancy wasn't alone. Standing right next to him was the most handsome-looking boy Summer had ever seen.

13

Summer blinked in amazement. He was still there. Dark, curling hair that just brushed his collar, high, well-defined cheekbones, a nice straight nose — all these thoughts assaulted the dumbfounded Summer. For over a year she had been the only person under the age of fifty at bingo night, and had every right to be surprised.

Who was he? she wondered. And why didn't she wear her blue skirt instead of her faded jeans, she lamented with a silent groan. And her hair! It was in a ponytail instead of down and curled. She looked positively juvenile.

The realization that she was actually standing there flash-frozen with her mouth wide open finally penetrated, and Summer struggled to regain some of her composure. It was easier said than done.

"Am I late, Mr. Clancy?" Good heavens, her voice sounded like a squeaky chair.

"Not to worry, dear," Mr. Clancy beamed. "Summer, I'd like you to meet Frank Marshall's grandson, David. David, this is Summer Matthews."

"Nice to meet you," Summer replied with as much dignity as she could muster. It was hard work; speech was a little difficult, for David had turned to smile at her and he had the most startling green eyes. He's beautiful, she thought, and I look like a frump.

"Hi," David said.

"You two take care of the customers while I make more coffee," Mr. Clancy said.

The next fifteen minutes were busy. Everyone was in a hurry to get their refreshments before the first round of bingo. Summer was relieved, she felt all tongue-tied and panicky. What would she talk about? Her mind spun with a multitude of questions she could ask him, but they all sounded like she was interviewing him for the school paper . . . not just talking.

Did other girls feel this awkward around boys? Summer wondered. Ann Logan would know just what to say, and be cute and coy at the same time.

"What school do you go to?" David had solved the problem.

Summer stopped wiping the counter top with the dishrag and turned to him. "Regis," she all but blurted. She lowered her voice so she wouldn't interfere with the bingo calling and continued. "And you?"

"Chalmers," David answered. Summer was impressed. Chalmers was a boys' prep school. No wonder she had never seen him before. "I'll be a senior next term. What about you?"

"Lowly sophomore," Summer replied with a grin. She hoped her dimple showed when she smiled. Regina had often said it was one of her best features. "We might as well sit down over there and wait for intermission," she added and gestured to the small card table set up against the back wall.

Neither said a word until they were facing each other across the table. Summer was still nervous; the palms of her hands were actually sweating and she fervently prayed that David wouldn't notice. She realized she was still holding the dishrag, and placed it on the table.

I'm being so silly, Summer decided. After all, he can't possibly be interested in me. A Chalmers boy, as handsome as David, and a *senior* to boot. . . . No, Summer was sure he must have a dozen girls interested in him. He was just being nice and polite while they worked together. For some reason, Summer relaxed. Since she didn't stand a chance with him, why try? She would just enjoy this evening and be herself. Besides, she really wasn't any good at gushing anyway. It wasn't her style.

The pressure was off. Summer found herself talking freely, telling David all about the coed school she attended. They discussed the merits and drawbacks of both schools. David seemed so relaxed, and actually looked like he was interested in what she had to say.

"Why are you here tonight?" Summer asked at one point. She decided she sounded too blunt, and hurried to add, "I mean, I come every Monday night and I was just wondering why I haven't seen you here before."

"This is my first time," David replied. "My grandfather has a heart condition and can't drive the car anymore, so I volunteered to bring him. He likes to play bingo."

"My grandfather loves bingo," Summer

said. "He plays at least twenty cards at a time," she exaggerated.

"So does my grandfather," David said and then chuckled. "Has your grandfather ever won?"

"No, but he says he's always close. Too close to give up," Summer replied. "I walk with him to the church every Monday night, rain or shine. He wouldn't miss bingo for anything," she confessed.

"Will you be here next Monday, helping out again?" David asked.

"Sure," Summer answered. "What about you? Will you be coming back?" she asked the question as casually as she could.

"If you're going to be here, I will be."

David seemed embarrassed at what he had just said, his cheeks actually tinged pink, and Summer's stomach did a double flip. "Yes, I'll be here," she answered demurely. Inside she was screaming with joy.

The rest of the evening went by in a blur. Before she knew it, it was time to collect her grandfather and start home. David offered to drive them but before Summer could agree on that plan, her grandfather stated that the walk was his only exercise. Summer hid her disappointment. She was on cloud nine. David had asked her for her phone number!

# _Two_

The next morning Summer was running late and had to race to get Michael ready for his swimming lesson. He looked terribly silly walking beside her in a lemon-yellow swimsuit and his red winter boots but Summer didn't have time to argue with him. At least he had promised to remove both the boots and the red towel when he was in the pool. Summer only had time to put on a pair of her mother's sunglasses and hope that no one recognized her.

They were standing on the corner of High Drive and Meyer Boulevard when Summer heard her name called. She recognized the singsong voice immediately. Ann Logan. So much for the disguise, Summer thought with a sigh. She removed the sunglasses and squinted at Ann.

"Summer, I'm so glad I spotted you," Ann said, leaning out of the window of her sports car. "I wanted to invite you to a little swim party I'm having next Wednesday. I do hope you can come," she giggled. "Of course, you'll have to bring a date," she added with a definite smirk, "but if you can't find one, call me and I'll see what I can do."

"I'm sure I can find a date, Ann. Thank you for inviting me," Summer said sweetly. She wanted to add, Why did you invite me?, but thought she knew that answer. Ann liked an audience to stand on the sidelines while she reigned as Miss Popularity with the boys.

The stoplight changed and Ann waved a dramatic farewell before gunning the motor. Both Summer and Michael watched her zoom off. Ann Logan was one of the few sophomores who had turned sixteen and had a driver's license. The sports car was a sweet-sixteen present from her parents. That was ironic, Summer decided, for there wasn't a darn thing sweet about Ann Logan.

"Come on, Michael," Summer snapped. She grabbed hold of his hand, sticky from the sucker he had just finished, and propelled him across the street. Ann Logan had a knack for putting Summer in a rotten mood.

"Slow down, Summer," Michael protested.

"Sorry," Summer replied when she realized Michael was literally running to keep up. She abruptly changed the pace to match his short-legged stride. They entered the park, dodging a couple of joggers as they made their way to the pool.

The water was going to be cold, Summer realized, but she had worn her swimsuit under her jeans and blouse anyway. A good swim would be invigorating, and since running into Ann Logan, it would be just the thing to rid Summer of the huge knot of tension settling in the base of her neck. The fact that the only reason Ann had invited her to the party was because she was sure Summer couldn't get a date, galled her. It galled her, and it hurt.

"Hi." The deep voice shocked Summer, and sent shivers of delight racing down her legs. It was David.

"David!" Summer exclaimed. "What are you doing here? I thought you were working." Yet even as she spoke, Summer took in his appearance hoping she wasn't gaping. He was wearing navy blue, very official-looking swim trunks. "You're the swimming instructor, aren't you?"

"How'd you guess?" David teased.

"My brother must be taking his lesson from you," Summer all but stammered.

It was too good to be true. She would get to see David every single day for the next two weeks.

While she spoke, Michael had edged behind her legs, peering out and up at David with obvious suspicion. Summer glanced down and immediately took in the expression. Michael was definitely having second thoughts.

She was about to drag him out from behind

her when David squatted down beside her, his face just inches from her little brother's. "Hi, there," he said. "You ready to learn how to swim, buddy?"

"No." The one word was issued into the back of Summer's kneecaps.

"Well, then, come and sit beside me on the side of the pool. You don't mind getting your feet wet, do you?"

"Do I have to get my face wet?" Michael asked with a frown.

"Not unless you want to," David replied.

Michael believed him. David looked up at Summer and winked. "Why don't you come back in half an hour?" he suggested, and before either Summer or Michael could argue the point, David had taken Michael's hand and was walking toward the pool.

"He can't swim at all," Summer yelled and then felt herself blush. She was sounding just like a mother hen!

David nodded so she knew he heard her. She waved and quickly turned to leave, before Michael decided to make a scene.

For the next half hour, Summer roamed the park. It seemed an eternity. She contemplated running home and changing into something more sophisticated. Or maybe she should let her hair out of the sloppy knot she had hurriedly twisted it into on top of her head, but discarded that idea. David would know she was interested in making a good impression on him if she did that, and even Summer knew one simply didn't act overly eager where boys were concerned. Regina said it scared them off.

The pool area was crowded with mothers and children when Summer returned. David praised Michael a great deal in front of Summer, and her little brother positively glowed. His hair was plastered back from his face, indicating that he had gotten more than his feet wet.

"It's good that Mike is learning to swim early. It's easier with his age group. The older ones get all uptight."

"Do you give group lessons, too?" Summer asked. "Or are they all individual lessons like Michael's?"

"He's my only single," David answered. "I have four groups. I'm finished by noon every day." He was so self-assured and confident, and there was a note of pride in his voice.

"Is this your first year teaching?" Summer asked.

"Can you tell?" Was there a tinge of vulnerability in his voice? Summer decided not. She smiled and shook her head. "You're very good with little kids."

Before David could reply, Summer prodded Michael into saying thank you and they turned to leave. From behind her she heard David whisper, "I'll call you later, okay?"

"That would be nice," Summer murmured in a soft voice. She strove to maintain a sophisticated attitude, holding her smile at a minimum when she glanced back at him. David didn't need to know she was bursting at the seams.

Summer began to pace back and forth in front of the phone. She was beginning to have great empathy with the animals who paced in their cages at the zoo. But at exactly five minutes after four, David called.

Over the phone David sounded very formal. "Hello, Summer? This is David Marshall, and I was wondering if you'd like to go to the movies with me tomorrow night? If you're busy maybe we could do it another time." Odd, but David sounded like he was out of breath.

"That would be great," Summer replied when David slowed down. She decided that playing hard to get would be stupid. She told him where she lived and agreed that seven o'clock would be a good time to be picked up.

"Ask him if he has any tall friends," Regina insisted when Summer told her the news. She sounded just as excited as Summer was but couldn't stay on the phone because her brother needed to use it.

"Come over and help me decide what to wear," Summer begged, and Regina, best friend that she was, didn't let her down.

"I'm leaving right this minute." Summer could always count on Regina!

By the time Regina arrived, Summer had three possible outfits displayed on the bed.

"It's definitely the blue dress," Regina declared. "It just matches the color of your eyes. You'll look super."

"I still can't believe . . ."

". . . he asked you out, right?" Regina finished for her.

"Wait until you meet him, Regina. He's . . . magnificent."

"Are you going to ask him to Ann's party?"

"I thought I would," Summer replied. "Why are you frowning? Don't you think it's a good idea?"

"Well, part of me does. I want to see the look on Ann's face when you show up with a Chalmers boy. She'll be green with envy. The other part of me says to keep your David as far away from Ann Logan as possible. Don't tempt fate."

"Well, I'm going to ask him," Summer decided. "Not every boy falls for her act. David is much too mature." Summer's voice sounded very sure, but a nagging worry was forming in the back of her head. She ignored her misgivings and squared her shoulders. "Didn't you say we all have the same equipment as Ann? Well, we just need to know how to use it like she does. David must like me a little, Regina, or he wouldn't have asked me out. Right?"

"Right!" Regina's enthusiastic reply was at odds with the frown wrinkling her brow.

"It's time to fight fire with fire," Summer said with false confidence.

"You're one hundred percent right," Regina declared. "I'm just a worry wart. Besides, I've seen Ann in action more than you have," she added.

"Think positive," Summer chanted. "I sound just like my dad." Both girls laughed. "He's right, you know," Summer continued. "It's time to give Ann Logan a little set down."

"Right!"

"We sound like a pep rally," Summer chuckled. "And I will ask David all about his friends, including their height."

"I asked Carl to Ann's party but he can't go," Regina said with a shrug. "He's going out of town."

"But you have to go to the party," Summer said.

"I will," Regina answered. "I'm going to make Gregg take me," she added. "That way I can really circulate. And besides, I wouldn't miss seeing . . ."

". . . Ann's face when David and I make our appearance?"

"Exactly!" Regina said.

It seemed to Summer that an entire lifetime passed before it was truly Wednesday night. She was dressed and ready to go a good hour before David was due. One final look in the hall mirror convinced her that there wasn't anything more she could do. She looked as good as she was ever going to look, which really wasn't all that bad, she decided with almost clinical detachment. For once her hair had decided to conform, falling in soft waves around her slender shoulders.

Summer had prepared her family as best she could. Luck was on her side. Grandfather had decided to return to the basement right after dinner and though she felt a little guilty, she sighed with relief. There was no telling just what her grandfather would do in front of David. And if he was in one of his teasing moods. . . . Summer shuddered to think of that possibility.

"Mother, I'll wait up here. Remember, you let David in and then call me, okay?"

"My, don't you look lovely," her mother said. "And don't worry. We'll all behave."

A short time later the door bell chimed. Summer stood at the top of the landing, carefully concealed behind one of her father's jungle plants, and waited. She didn't want to appear overly eager. She would wait until her mother called her, then count to ten, and then, she would slowly descend, her head held high, her eyes —

"Michael, tell this young man what you would be if you weren't Irish."

"A-a-a-shamed," squealed her little brother.

The alarm bell inside Summer's head was ringing loud and clear. Her grandfather was entertaining David!

Summer automatically responded. She almost tripped over her own feet in her haste to get downstairs, sounding very much like an elephant in tap shoes on the uncarpeted steps, and unfortunately, David saw and heard the whole thing.

"Hello, David," she rushed. "I see you've met the family. Well, we better leave now."

"Summer, where're your manners?" her father said from behind. "Ask the young man to sit and talk for a few minutes."

It couldn't be avoided. Summer led David to the sofa and sat down next to him. Grandfather perched on the arm of the chair Summer's mother was sitting in. Her father gave her a smile of encouragement and sat down in his favorite leather chair. He didn't seem to notice that he was holding a potted plant in his lap, Summer decided, but she was sure David must have thought that a bit strange.

"Michael tells us you're a fine swimming instructor," her father began.

"I did not," Michael interrupted but quickly fell silent when he caught Summer's glare.

"Of course you did, son," her father continued in a smooth voice. "Do you enjoy teaching, David?"

"Oh, yes, sir," David replied. "And Mike is going to be a great swimmer, aren't you?"

"Yep," Michael responded.

"Well, I best be getting back to the basement, now that I've met your young man," Grandfather bellowed. "I'm just putting the finishing touches on my latest invention," he confided to David in a conspiratorial and very loud whisper.

Don't ask, oh please, don't ask, Summer prayed.

"What is it you're working on, sir?" David asked.

"A remote-control, self-cleaning birdbath."

David, bless his heart, didn't bat an eye. "Sounds like a useful gadget," was all he said.

"What time are you planning on bringing my little girl home?" her father asked. Summer hated it when he called her his little girl, and almost screamed in frustration. She moved slightly and became aware of a bulge right under her right leg. It was most probably a toy, her mother's keys or Grandpa's dentures. Summer didn't want to know what it was. Slowly sliding her hand along the side of her skirt, she pushed the item between the cushions and only then let out the breath she had been holding.

"The movie gets out at ten and I thought Summer and I could get a bite to eat after that. Would eleven-thirty be all right?" David's voice was so calm and reassuring! Summer stole a quick glance at him before turning back to her father. He was frowning in absolute concentration, as if David had just asked him to explain the national debt.

"Normally our Summer has to be in by eleven," he stated, "but I'll make an exception this time. Eleven-thirty should give you enough time for a snack, don't you think?"

"Yes, sir, and thank you," David said. He turned to Summer and grinned. "We better get going or we'll be late."

"You got any gum?" Michael suddenly demanded. He wrapped his arms around David's kneecaps, making it impossible for David to stand up.

"Michael, it isn't proper to ask for things," Summer stammered. "And get your hands off David. You're all grimy." Summer shot her mother a pleading look.

"Sure I do, Mike," David replied. He peeled Michael from him and stood up. Reaching into his pant's pocket, he extracted a pack of Juicy Fruit and offered a stick to Michael.

Michael was impressed. Juicy Fruit was one of his favorites.

"Tell David 'thank you,'" their mother suggested with a smile.

The ordeal was finally over. Summer was so relieved she didn't have time to worry about how close she should sit next to David in the car.

Neither said a word until they were on their way to the movie theater.

"Your family is nice," David said.

You mean crazy, don't you? Summer wanted to say but didn't. "Thank you," she substituted instead. "Do you have any brothers or sisters?"

"No," David answered. "I'm an only child. Sometimes I wish I had a brother or a sister. Be kind of neat to share things with someone at home."

"Michael isn't into sharing yet," Summer said with a smile.

"He looks like the kind of kid who's into everything," David said with a chuckle. "You know, it took me ten minutes just to talk him into taking his boots off at the pool today."

"Yes, well . . . he kind of identifies with Superman," Summer answered. "Mom says it's a stage he's going through."

"Were your parents surprised when Mike came along?"

Summer thought that question over, trying to figure out how she was going to answer that one, when David said, "Look, I shouldn't have asked such a personal question. It's just that they seem a little . . ."

"Old?" Summer suggested.

"Yeah, a little bit older than most parents with little kids. I know it's none of my business but I really think it's neat. Mike's a real character."

"It's okay, it's not a personal question. It's just kind of weird, that's all. Mom and Dad were married for five years before I was born, and then Mom was told she couldn't have any more children. I was an only child for twelve years and then Michael came along. Everyone was really surprised. It was a big adjustment."

"It must have been strange to have a baby around all of a sudden," David said.

"Mom and Dad were thrilled, but I—" Summer was suddenly embarrassed, remembering how put-out she was the entire time her mother was carrying Michael. Embarrassed and a little ashamed. "I acted like a spoiled brat," Summer admitted and promptly blushed with her admission. Why in heaven's name was she telling David all this? she asked herself. He couldn't possibly be interested in her family.

"Well, it had to be hard on you, what with all the changes," David said. He burst into laughter, saw Summer's puzzled expression, and hurried to add, "Changes, get it? Diapers?" He continued to chuckle, immensely pleased with his little pun.

"Corny, David," Summer replied, shaking her head. "Definitely corny."

"Sorry," David answered, but the lopsided grin he displayed contradicted his apology.

"You know, I can't imagine *not* having Michael around now, or Grandfather, for that matter. He moved in last year, after Grandmother died."

"He seems real nice," David said.

"Tell me about your family," Summer suggested.

"Not much to tell," David replied. "Dad's an accountant and Mom stays home most of the time."

"What about you? Do you know what you want to do when you finish school?"

"Not really. Sometimes I think I want to be a doctor but you have to be real good in science and I'm just average."

David found a place to park a block away from the theater. When Summer got out of the car, he took hold of her hand and held it until they reached the entrance. Neither spoke, but it was a comfortable silence. Summer was trying to memorize everything David said so she could tell Regina, and wanted to be witty and interesting at the same time. It was an exhausting task! She felt herself tense up again, and took a deep breath. "Do you play any sports?" she heard herself ask.

"Sure," David answered. "Lots of soccer and a little baseball. What about you?"

"I was on a softball team," Summer said, and that much was true. She just didn't mention that she was eight years old at the time, and signed up to play only because of the powder-blue uniforms the girls got to wear.

"What about tennis?" David asked. "I just got a new racket but I haven't played much."

"I've only played a couple of times," Summer answered. "I don't even know all the rules."

"Want to set up a game for tomorrow afternoon, around four? It shouldn't be too hot then," David said.

"I wish I could," Summer said, crossing her fingers. "But I have to watch Michael. Mom doesn't get home from the flower shop until five." Summer was pleased that David wanted to see her again, but felt that she would make a complete fool of herself if she tried to play tennis. She did own a tennis racket, but only because Regina had given her one two summers ago when Regina had a crush on the tennis coach. They never actually played, just circled the tennis courts a couple of times a day in their outfits, hoping to catch the coach's eye.

"Bring him with you," David said. "He can play on the swings. What do you say?"

David sounded so eager and enthusiastic. Summer decided she would have to agree. If she didn't, David might think she didn't want to be with him.

"Okay, David, but I better warn you. With Michael along, we won't get much tennis played."

"No problem," David said. "Come on, let's get some popcorn."

It wasn't until they were seated in the middle of the crowded theater and the lights were fading that Summer thought to ask what movie they were going to see.

"It's a comedy," David explained. "My friend Charlie said it was real funny."

"Is he tall?" Summer asked the question before she could stop herself.

"Pardon me?" David looked puzzled and leaned down until his forehead was just inches from Summer's upturned face. His aftershave smelled so clean and fresh and spicy, and Summer hoped he could smell her perfume.

"Oh, nothing," Summer mumbled. She would work on finding a date for Regina later.

Summer enjoyed the movie, but David

*really* enjoyed it! His laughter, full and completely uninhibited, laced with an appreciative snort every now and then, drew stares from the people around them, but Summer didn't mind at all. The fact that he was so relaxed and obviously enjoying himself pleased her. When he finished his extra-large tub of popcorn, he draped his arm around her shoulders like it was the most natural thing to do. Summer felt like purring with contentment.

The movie ended all too soon as far as Summer was concerned. David suggested they go get hamburgers and Summer readily agreed. She was glad he didn't suggest the Pizza Paddle because she didn't want to share him with any of her friends just yet. That would come soon enough, at Ann Logan's party . . . if she could get her nerve up to ask him.

"I've never known anyone named Summer," David said on the way home. "Is it a family name?"

"No." Summer answered. "Mom just liked it. Dad wanted to name me after a flower, but Mom won out." Summer didn't add that her father still occasionally called her Rosebud when he was in a teasing mood. That information came under the heading of boring family trivia.

"I like your name. It suits you."

Summer wasn't sure what David meant, but knew that he was giving her a compliment. She was glad her name was Summer.

It wasn't until they were saying good-night on the front porch that Summer found enough courage to ask David to be her date for Ann Logan's party. "I had a wonderful time, David. Thank you for inviting me," she whispered. The noise from the television was blaring through the screen door and Summer didn't want to alert her parents to the fact that they were home.

"I'll pick you up at four tomorrow, okay?" David asked just as softly.

"Fine," Summer answered. It was now or never. "David, a friend of mine — well, she really isn't a friend, she's a classmate — and she's having this swim party next Wednesday night. We're supposed to bring dates and I was wondering if you would like to go with me." The last was blurted out but Summer didn't care. David was smiling and nodding. He really seemed pleased she had asked him.

"Sure," he answered. "We can talk about the time and all that tomorrow, okay?"

"Okay," Summer replied.

David put his hands on Summer's shoulders and leaned down toward her. "Summer, is that you?" Her father's voice surprised Summer and she jumped. David let go of her shoulders and took a step backwards. Both she and David began to laugh, and everything was just fine.

"Yes, Dad," Summer called. "I'll be right in."

She watched David walk down the steps

before turning to go into the house.

"See you tomorrow," David called over his shoulder.

"Did you have a good time, sweetheart?" her father asked.

"Just fine, Daddy," Summer answered. "Just fine."

# Three

Regina was sitting on the porch steps when Summer returned from the park with a water-logged Michael in tow. "How'd your swimming lesson go, Mike?" Regina asked.

"I got my face wet," Michael answered as he threw himself on Regina's lap. He was happy to see Regina and grinned up at her.

Summer settled next to the pair on the top step and gave Regina a blow-by-blow description of her date with David.

"He sounds wonderful," Regina sighed. "What about his friends? Any tall ones?"

"He mentioned a boy named Charlie. I'll ask all the necessary questions when we play tennis today."

"Just don't be too eager when you tell him about me. And *don't* say I've got a great personality," Regina warned. "He'll think I'm a dog. And be casual about it. If the opportunity doesn't come up, wait until Ann's party and then ask him."

"Okay, okay," Summer said. "Regina, I *do* know how to be tactful."

Summer was so excited about David, she felt like jumping up and doing a little jig just like Michael did when he was told he was going to get some special treat. "Oh Regina, David is almost perfect. He does have one little, tiny flaw, though," Summer began.

"What?" Regina asked.

"You'll think I'm being silly. . . ."

"So?"

"Well, he tells these really terrible jokes. I mean, they aren't funny at all, but he thinks they are. He laughs so hard after he tells the punch line that his shoulders shake and I don't think he even notices that I'm not laughing. Honestly, Regina, he told one bad joke after another all the way home. I think he has a hidden ambition to be a stand-up comic," Summer concluded.

"That's not such a bad flaw," Regina said. "I thought you were going to tell me something gross. Now drooling, twitching, scratching all the time. . . . Those are definite flaws."

"Be serious," Summer demanded.

"Okay," Regina replied. "But if telling bad jokes is David's only flaw, then I still say he's perfect. At least he has a sense of humor."

"You're right. He *is* perfect." Summer agreed. "Now let's get down to business,

Regina. How in heaven's name am I going to learn to play tennis before four o'clock?"

David was prompt. At exactly four o'clock he knocked on the screen door. He was also thoughtful. He produced an entire pack of Juicy Fruit gum and handed it to Michael, who tore immediately into the package with squeals of delight.

"Want to walk to the park?" David asked. "It's only a couple of blocks from here."

"Sure," Summer agreed.

"Hey, Mike, is that a new towel you're wearing?" David looked like he was about to laugh but Michael didn't seem to care or notice that David was teasing him. He was too busy stuffing sticks of gum into his mouth.

"It's my cape," Michael explained between bites.

"Come on, Michael, it's time to leave," Summer called after him.

"I need my glasses Grandpa gave me," Michael yelled back. He appeared a minute later with a pair of white children's sunglasses perched on his nose.

"Want to ride on my shoulders to the park, Superman?" David asked.

When Michael nodded, David lifted him up and placed him on his shoulders. Michael locked his boots under David's chin.

"David, you're really good with kids," Summer said. She was secretly pleased that David wasn't embarrassed by Michael's attire. "You take things in stride."

"Thanks. I like kids, they're so natural and honest. You always know where you stand with them."

"That's certainly true of Michael," Summer said.

David laughed. "There's a swing set right next to the tennis courts. We'll be able to keep an eye on Superman while we play."

Summer found herself getting all nervous again. "Remember, I don't know much about the game," she said. "Oh . . . maybe when we get there you could find someone else to play with, and Michael and I could watch you. I mean, well . . . I wouldn't want to slow you down."

"I thought you said you've played before," David said while he readjusted Michael on his shoulders.

I would have said anything to go out with you, Summer felt like saying. But after his remarks about liking Michael because he was so open and honest, Summer instinctively felt that telling him the truth wasn't such a hot idea. "I have played," she blatantly lied, "but it was years and years ago. I'm not too coordinated when it comes to playing tennis. Maybe you could give me a few pointers."

David was watching her closely so she tried to bat her eyelashes as Regina had instructed her, hoping she looked innocent and cute at the same time.

"Got something in your eye?" David asked,

leaning down to have a closer look.

Summer immediately quit blinking and shook her head. So much for cute!

"Don't worry," David advised, changing the subject back to tennis. "I'll be glad to teach you. I'm not very good either. We'll just take it slow and easy."

Famous last words, Summer concluded an hour later. It had started out easy enough. Michael cooperated by playing on the swings with a couple of older boys. Summer was convinced that she was putting on quite a show, running like a graceful ballerina all over her side of the court. She even managed a few dainty back kicks and one rather spectacular spin. She missed hitting the ball, of course, but she was close to it. Acting like she knew what she was doing was hard, exhausting work, she decided. Exhausting, but well worth it. David *had* to be impressed! Summer certainly was.

"Okay, Summer," David yelled. "That's enough warm-up. Let's play a game now."

She knew her mouth fell open, and she felt her knees try to buckle on her. What have we been doing for the past hour? she wanted to ask, but she was panting too hard.

"You serve first," David instructed. He was bouncing a tennis ball like a pancake on a frying pan, and looked completely relaxed.

Summer gritted her teeth, smiled, and nodded.

Summer glanced over at Michael, hoping she could use him as an excuse, but the little boy was calmly sitting on a swing, waiting for one of his new friends to give him a push.

The fates were against her! Summer was good and stuck, and she knew it. Taking a deep breath, she picked up a bright yellow tennis ball, gave it a good glare, and then imitated what she thought was a pretty good serve. It jammed into the tennis net, and David promptly yelled, "Fault!"

"You don't have to be so critical," Summer muttered under her breath. She smiled at David and picked up another ball, wiped the sweat from her forehead with the back of her hand, and served again. "Double fault," David yelled.

Summer felt like a three-day-old fish, spoiling fast. Her perky ponytail had definitely lost its perk, her blue blouse was stuck to her shoulder blades, and her tennis knee-high socks were losing their elasticity. In short, she was a mess.

And it was all downhill after that. David was patient as he yelled encouragement and suggestions. He tried to keep a straight face when Summer tripped over her tennis racket and landed on her backside, and even jumped over the tennis net to help her to her feet. However, when, a few minutes later, she crashed into the net, he had to turn his back and Summer could hear a few choked sounds coming from his direction. Summer glared at the back of him, noting that his shoulders were shaking.

She stood up and squared her shoulders,

aching from head to toe. When David turned around, Summer yelled, "And just what is so funny?" David didn't answer, and Summer, knowing in her heart that he would never, ever ask her out again, got good and angry. "Look David, I told you I wasn't good at tennis!" She folded her arms in front of her and wacked her elbow with the tennis racket she forgot she was holding.

David jumped over the net again and jogged toward her. Summer noticed that there wasn't an ounce of sweat on him. Every hair was still in place on the top of his beautiful head. He was grinning like crazy, and Summer felt her frustration slip away. "I played the best game I could," she explained. "What more can I tell you?" she added, extending her hands.

David jumped out of the way of her racket in the nick of time and then grabbed it from her. "I never realized that a tennis racket could be a lethal weapon," David said, chuckling, "until today."

"Very funny," Summer replied. She looked down at her knee-highs, now firmly anchored around her ankles.

David continued to chuckle and threw his arm around her shoulders. "I don't think I've ever had such a great time playing tennis. You're something else."

"I try," Summer answered. "At least *I* didn't broadcast to the whole world every time *you* messed up," she added.

"What?" David sounded confused.

"You didn't hear me scream 'Fault' at you, did you?" Summer said. "It really isn't very polite to point out another person's faults, you know."

"Summer, I wasn't criticizing you," David stammered. He started laughing again and Summer shook her head in exasperation.

He waited until he regained some control and then said, "In tennis, saying 'Fault' isn't criticism. It's just a way of keeping score. You'll learn all that stuff when we play more."

"You mean you want to play again?" Summer asked.

"Are you kidding? We've got to play again. I've had a great time," David said. "And you've got potential, Summer. Really," he added when she shook her head.

Summer could not contain her amazement. He really sounded like he meant what he was saying.

"You really want to try it again sometime?" she asked, knowing she sounded eager and not caring at all.

"Of course," David replied enthusiastically. "Before you know it, we'll be partners and playing in tournaments."

"Don't get your hopes up, David," Summer replied, grinning. "What you see is what you've got."

"I like what I see," David said, giving her shoulder a squeeze.

Before she had a chance to answer, Michael came running toward them. "Summer, I'm tired," he whined. "I want to go home right now!"

"I guess I should get going, too," David said.

"I had a wonderful time," Summer said. She helped David pick up the duffle bag and the rackets and didn't mind at all when he took hold of her hand.

"So did I," David said softly. "I won't be able to take you out until the swim party," David said as they started walking again.

Summer must have looked disappointed, she decided, because David hurried to add, "I'll see you at Mike's swim lessons, though, won't I?"

"Sure," Summer answered, smiling.

"And I'll call you, okay?"

"Fine."

David squeezed her hand and Summer felt her heart pick up a beat. She was so happy she thought she was in heaven!

# *F*our

Time dragged; time sped. One minute it seemed an eternity before Ann Logan's party, and the next, Summer was ready to go. David was picking her up at six, but Summer was ready by five. She had to be. She would need the extra hour to rehearse the family. A queasy feeling lodged itself in her stomach as she sought out her mother. She wasn't sure if she was nervous about the party or about her family. Probably a little of both, she decided.

"My, don't you look lovely, dear. Since you're ready to go, why don't you give me a hand and set the table?"

"Mother, plan on eating right at six, okay?" Summer hoped that everyone would have their mouths full of casserole and not be able to do more than wave when David arrived.

"Maybe I'll wait for David on the porch,"

Summer suggested once she had finished with the table.

"Don't be silly," her father admonished from behind the evening paper.

"You'll look a bit eager, don't you think?" her mother called from the dining room.

There was truth in that, Summer decided.

"Well, don't make us stay and visit again, Daddy, okay?" Please, Dad, she silently prayed, try to understand how nervous I am.

"All right, Rosebud. Don't worry so. It will be fine. You'll see. We'll all behave." Her father's face was still hidden behind the paper, but Summer knew he was smiling. She could hear the teasing tone in his voice.

"And, Daddy? Please don't call me Rosebud in front of David," Summer said. "That's just for family," she added in case she'd hurt his feelings.

When Summer opened the screen door for David, everyone but Grandfather was seated at the dining room table. They all appeared calm and decidedly normal as they greeted David. It was too good to be true. Even Grandfather cooperated — although he wasn't aware of that fact — by staying in the basement.

Summer had just picked up her purse and turned to walk toward the front door when *it* happened. The sudden, grinding *explosion* of noise literally shook the rafters. A lesser person might have thought a jet had just landed in the living room, but not Summer. She knew better.

David jumped and then grabbed Summer by the shoulders, pulling her to his side as if he would protect her. Summer sighed in defeat. She was vaguely aware of the iced-tea glasses rattling on the table, Michael's delighted yelps, and David's horrified expression.

Before her father could investigate the matter, Summer noticed that he was calmly folding his napkin with that resigned expression on his face, and before she could propel David out the front door, a runaway vacuum cleaner whizzed right past them, crashed into the china cabinet, turned, and whizzed past them again. It was like watching a tennis tournament, everyone frozen in place with only their heads moving back and forth as they followed the progress of the vacuum. Its speed defied all the laws of science, including the law of gravity, when it suddenly launched itself halfway up the living room wall, and if Summer had so much as blinked, she would have missed the entire show. A resounding crash, and it was over. The vacuum lay in a heap and everyone stared at it a long while. Silence reigned supreme.

"Just needs a few minor adjustments." The bellow came from the basement doorway, and everyone automatically turned to stare at Grandfather. He wore a sheepish grin, and held a remote control device in his hand.

Could someone die of embarrassment? Summer was sure she was about to be the first. She couldn't look at David. He still held her in a possessive grip, as if he was too stunned to move. The low rumble in his chest alerted her that he still lived. David was trying hard not to laugh.

"You two better get going. Enjoy yourselves," Summer's father called. He was back at the dinner table, calmly scooping tuna casserole onto his plate as if nothing out of the ordinary had happened.

She had to lead David to the car. "It's okay, you can laugh." Summer placed her towel and swim suit between them on the front seat, folded her hands in her lap, and looked straight ahead.

David was very obliging. He laughed until tears ran down his cheeks. It soon became infectious. Summer finally laughed along with him. It was heady relief from a bad case of nerves. He may never ask me out again, but at least he's still taking me to the party, Summer thought. Not too many boys had the stamina — or courage — to actually date someone from a loony-tune family.

"That was really something," David said when he calmed down. "Do you think your grandfather would let me help him with his work sometime? I wouldn't get in the way, and I'd do whatever he told me to do. I'm good with electronic stuff."

Summer was too shocked to reply.

"Will you ask him? Please?"

David was serious! He wasn't laughing *at* Grandfather, and really wanted to help him.

"Sure," Summer stammered. "I think he'd like that."

The party was in full swing when she and David arrived. The look on Ann Logan's face was priceless! She batted her eyelashes furiously until Summer was sure David thought Ann had a bad tic!

David didn't know a soul when they arrived, but within fifteen minutes he was eagerly discussing the coming football season with Regina's brother.

Where was Regina? Summer hunted inside for her a good five minutes and started back toward the pool when she finally spotted her. Regina was standing near the cabana and something was very, very wrong. The tightly clenched fists and the furious expression on Regina's face shocked her. Summer knew that look! Regina was going to make a scene. Having recognized the signs, Summer immediately went into action. She grabbed her friend's arm in a very unfeminine grip and literally propelled her around the crowded poolside, oblivious to the strange stares directed her way. She didn't stop until she had maneuvered Regina onto a secluded redwood deck on the side of the house.

"What in heaven's name is the matter with you?" Summer whispered frantically. One look at her friend's normally glowing complexion, now a definite three shades lighter, convinced Summer of the gravity of the situation. "You look like a vampire attacked you."

"He's here." The words were no more than a ragged whisper, but Summer caught them just the same. She understood Regina's mumblings.

"Who?"

"Carl, that's who."

"Carl? Here?" Incredulity raised Summer's own voice an octave. "Impossible."

"I'm telling you, he's here. I just saw him with Marilyn Nordstrom," Regina insisted emphatically. "And he told me he was going out of town!"

"Nonsense," Summer muttered. "You're seeing things. He's out of town, just like he told you."

The chilling look Regina shot her told Summer to revise her logic. She turned and edged around the corner of the yard. Quickly she scanned the area, finding the object of her friend's hysteria standing by the diving board.

"That creep."

Regina was too unglued to reply, shaking like a cube of Jell-O, much to Summer's disgust. Her tall, willowy friend was shrinking before her eyes. It was time to get her spine rigid again.

"Okay, what's our plan? What are we going to do about it?"

Summer waited for a response but gave up after a long minute. Regina's dark brown eyes seemed to look right through her, so lost was she in her misery. "So, my dear Watson," Summer continued in her best Sherlock

Holmes' voice, "it's quite elementary. We ignore him. Right?"

"Wrong!" Regina whispered in a tight, flat voice. Her pain was almost visible now, slapping like a cresting wave between them. "I'm going home."

Summer thought quickly. What Regina needed was a little reverse psychology. "You're right. You should just sneak out the side door and go home. It would take too much courage to stay and ignore Carl and pretend it doesn't matter. Even though no one knows you invited him. Still . . . I don't blame you. . . ."

"No way. I'm not sneaking anywhere. I'm staying," Regina said.

Summer's head snapped up at the sound of steel in her friend's voice. "That's the spirit. You stick with David and me and we'll circulate. Don't even look at Carl once. Pretend he doesn't exist. And you were right," she added as an afterthought. "He does lisp."

"Come on. I want to meet David. Then let's impress the heck out of everyone and do some laps in the pool."

Side by side, the two girls strolled toward the pool. Suddenly Summer stopped in her tracks.

"I should have known," she said.

"What?" Regina asked.

"Find Ann Logan and you'll find my date. She's draped all over him."

Regina spotted Ann and gave the couple a

long look. She turned back to Summer and said, "David is gorgeous."

"Ann certainly thinks so. It was a bad idea to bring David. I never should have let you talk me into it," Summer muttered in a defeated voice.

"*I* talked you into it? It was all your idea, remember? Now shape up. You sound like you just lost the war, and the first battle hasn't even begun."

She's right, Summer thought. "Come on Regina. I'll introduce you to David."

David looked happy to see Summer. Ann didn't look as pleased and that fact made Summer very happy. She quickly introduced Regina to David, and while they talked, she considered one idea after another to get Ann's hand off David's arm.

"David, want to swim a couple of laps with me?" Summer suddenly asked.

"Why, Summer, do you really swim?" Ann coyly inquired.

"Of course she does," Regina snapped. "Summer's extremely athletic. She might even go out for the swim team next year, if it doesn't interfere with . . . with her running schedule."

What running schedule? Summer wanted to ask. Regina was being a little too enthusiastic.

"Do you run?" David seemed impressed.

Before Summer could open her mouth, Regina answered for her. "Does she run! At least ten miles every single morning. You should see her David. She's like a . . . gazelle."

The none-too-gentle nudge Summer gave Regina finally stopped her praise.

"I run, too. Have you entered any races?" David pulled away from Ann and came to stand just inches from Summer. He seemed excited. "I'm glad you don't just jog," he he added with a trace of disgust. Obviously there was a difference between the two, but for the life of her, Summer didn't have a clue as to what that would be.

"No . . . no, I've never entered any races." That much was true, Summer admitted. She just didn't bother to add that she hadn't run as far as the mailbox in front of her house to her porch steps in all her life, let alone the outrageous ten miles Regina had boasted. After all, the little "fabrication" had served its purpose. Summer now had David's undivided attention — not Ann Logan.

"Let's run together sometime," David said with a great deal of gusto.

"Oh, I don't think so, David," Summer replied with a sugar-sweet smile. "I usually run early in the morning, before my parents leave for the flower shop, and I sort of use that time to . . . contemplate. You know, think things over. I wouldn't be good company."

Summer noticed that Ann was looking at her with a strange expression on her face. David acted like he was going to argue the point so Summer swiftly changed the subject. "Let's swim before the food is ready, okay?"

David agreed and left to change into his swim suit. Summer waited until Ann wandered off and then turned to a guilty-looking Regina. She rolled her eyes heavenward and groaned. "A gazelle?" she whispered. "I run like a gazelle?"

"I could have said a greyhound," Regina began to tell her.

"You should have said *snail*. That was a close one, Regina. I don't think Ann believed a word of it, either. You and your big mouth."

"Well, it worked, didn't it? Who cares if Ann believed us or not? I got David away from her, didn't I?" Regina pointed out.

It was useless to argue with Regina. "Come on, let's swim."

"Don't look so upset, Summer. So I lied a little. What's the big deal?"

"Okay," Summer placated. "You're absolutely right. There was no harm done. What can happen?" She grinned at Regina and both girls suddenly started to laugh. Arms linked together, they chuckled all the way to the pool.


"Brace yourself." The furious warning came from Regina who was waiting outside the bathroom door when Summer emerged. Regina resembled a tightly coiled Slinky, just ready to explode into motion. Summer almost dropped her wet bathing suit and frowned in exasperation.

"What happened?"

55

"You aren't going to take this well. . . ." Regina stalled.

"Tell me, Regina. Just tell me," Summer implored.

"I'll tell you, Summer."

Summer and Regina turned as one to face Ann Logan. David was standing right behind good old Ann, beaming. "I've just had the most splended idea and David is *so* excited about it."

"What might that be?" Summer asked with false cheerfulness. Any idea of Ann's had to be a lulu.

"Why, the Regis Run For Charity! Daddy's in charge of the event this year, you know," Ann told her.

No, Summer didn't know, and she didn't care. Things were taking a very bad turn and she didn't like where this was all leading.

"I've signed us up, Summer. Okay?" David asked in an eager voice. Good heavens, he looked so proud of himself. Summer had the almost uncontrollable urge to throw a tantrum, after she pulled Ann's eyelashes out, one by one.

She opened her mouth to say something but no words came out. Regina elbowed her in the ribs and then began chattering. Talking nonstop was one of Regina's biggest pluses, Summer thought.

"It's only *six* miles, Summer, and it's not for two whole months." Regina's eyes were flashing the message that they had plenty of time to figure something out, Summer decided.

Summer *hated* what was happening! She felt like a puppet being manipulated by Regina and David and Ann.

"Six miles?" Summer's voice sounded like she had a bad case of laryngitis. Ann Logan folded her arms and smiled that satisfied, *knowing* smile. That tipped the scales. Summer only wanted to wipe that Cheshire cat's grin off Ann's face. Nothing else mattered. "Only six miles?" she repeated. Good! Her voice held just the right tinge of disappointment and Summer had the wonderful satisfaction of seeing indecision appear for a fleeting second in Ann Logan's baby blues. It was almost worth it.

"I already paid our fees," David explained. "Mr. Logan says we're the first entries."

"Terrific," Summer replied, looking at Regina.

"It's for charity but there's a first-place cash prize for the winning boy and girl. We won't be running against each other, Summer." David's voice stressed the last sentence.

"How much?" Regina demanded.

"Five hundred dollars," David answered.

"Wow," Regina said with an unladylike whistle.

"Time to eat," Ann announced to everyone and then turned to Summer with a purely hateful gleam in her eyes. "Summer, why didn't you tell me you were such a . . . jock?"

# $F$*ive*

The best course of action was to tell David the truth. Summer was convinced that he would understand how she got a little carried away on the spur of the moment. That would be the sensible thing to do. Still, a nagging uncertainty remained. In order to explain her rash behavior, she would have to voice her insecurity where Ann Logan was concerned. Did boys understand such feelings? Summer doubted that.

Once Ann left them alone, she and David really did have a good time at the party. Summer knew she was being envied by all the girls, and she loved every minute of it. After all, David was *her* date and he seemed to be having a good time. If only he wouldn't talk so much about the stupid race.

When they finished eating, David took hold of her hand and pulled her over to a lounge chair. Everyone else was still eating, and she and David were all alone, sitting side by side. He continued holding her hand, rubbing her palm with his thumb as he watched the crowd of people.

"Do you like my friends?" Summer asked.

"All but that Terry guy. He's kind of a jerk," David said.

Summer asked, "Why do you think so?"

"He was telling a group of girls about all the trophies he's won in football," David answered. "It sounded like he was exaggerating."

"Well," Summer said, "he probably was exaggerating a little to get the girls' attention."

"You shouldn't lie, no matter what," David answered. His statement was so firm. A knot was forming in Summer's stomach and she wished she hadn't eaten anything. It would really be tacky to throw up on her third — and probably her last — date with the boy of her dreams.

"You place great stock in honesty, don't you?" Summer asked, already knowing the answer.

"Yeah," David answered. "You feel like swimming again?"

I feel like drowning myself, Summer wanted to answer. "No, I'm waterlogged," she said instead.

"Let's get our stuff and go for a drive before you have to be home, okay? Just the two of us," David whispered.

"Okay," Summer answered, smiling. Why

not, she asked herself. She might as well have one, wonderful, romantic evening with David before he dropped her for good. When he found out she was nothing but a lying, deceiving creep, he would never talk to her again!

She sighed with frustration as she gathered her towel and swim suit. David went to thank Ann for inviting them, and Summer trailed behind, stopping to say good-bye to Regina and Gregg. When she caught up with David, Ann was beside him, doubled over in laughter. David looked like the cat that ate the canary.

"What's so funny, Ann?" Summer asked, trying to keep the irritation out of her voice.

"David!" Ann replied, wiping the tears from her eyes with a lacy bit of froth. She was the only girl Summer knew who carried around a real hankie. Everyone else used tissues, but not Ann. Probably had perfume on it, too, Summer decided, after she watched Ann wave it in front of David's nose a couple of times. "He's just been telling me the funniest joke."

So that was why David looked so pleased, Summer thought. Ann laughed at his jokes. Chalk one up for Ann, Summer thought with another sigh. She certainly did know how to make a boy feel good. Summer decided that she was batting zero in that department. She hadn't laughed at any of his jokes, didn't think they were the least bit funny, and had lied through her teeth about running. And

David had to be such a fanatic about telling the truth! What a mess I've gotten myself into, Summer thought. What a colossal mess!

"Why are you frowning?" David asked on the way to the car.

Tell him now, an inner voice demanded. Just explain it was all a silly mistake! Maybe he'll forgive you.

"Nothing," Summer whispered. "I'm just relaxing," she lied.

David took hold of her hand and gave it a gentle squeeze.

They drove around the park in comfortable silence and then stopped at Dairy Delight. Summer sipped a chocolate malted and watched David down two double-dip hot fudge specials.

They talked about his family and hers on the way home. All too soon they were parked in front of Summer's house. It was time to end the charade, Summer decided. She was going to tell him the truth, go inside, and cry herself to sleep.

"David, about the race. . . ."

He responded by giving her his full attention and his heart-stopping smile. Summer promptly lost her train of thought, noticing for the first time the tiny silver flecks in his eyes. And his teeth, they were so white and even — a dentist's dream, Summer thought.

"I'm really excited about it," David said. "Are you sure you don't want to run with me every day? We could pace each other and — "

"No," Summer interrupted, inwardly

grimacing at the sound of panic in her voice. Coward, she berated herself. "I do better when I'm alone," she lied. Disgusting, she thought. I am a disgusting, lying. . . . "I'd better go inside," she added. "It's late and I like to get up and uh . . . exercise first thing in the morning."

"I had a good time, tonight, Summer. Thank you for inviting me," David said. He carried her towel to the front door and handed it to her. "I'll call you tomorrow, after work."

"Fine," Summer whispered. She knew he was going to kiss her and tilted her head back. He didn't disappoint her. The first touch of his lips sent tremors racing down her legs. It was a perfect kiss, not awkward or clumsy.

After David left, Summer made it to her bedroom. She wasn't sure if she walked or floated up the stairs. She was in love! For the first time in her life she knew what loving someone was all about. It was heaven and it was torture! The race! She had lied to David. He would find out soon enough, when she fell flat on her face after the first twenty paces, and then what would he think of her? How could he possibly love a lying, no-good cheat?

It would be so easy to just blame Regina, but Summer was honest enough with herself to admit that she had willingly gone along with the fabrication.

The problem had to have a solution. Didn't

Grandpa say that often enough? A good night's sleep and Summer would be clear-headed. Answers would come with the morning dew. On that positive thought, Summer went to bed, hugging her pillow tightly, pretending it was David.

So much for positive thinking, Summer muttered the following morning. She had been up for hours and still not a single plan of action presented itself. Regina's phone call didn't help matters. She had actually suggested that Summer start shopping for an outfit to wear to the dumb race!

In desperation Summer decided to confide in her grandfather. She knew he would never betray her confidence. Besides, he would probably forget what she told him before the day was out. And, more importantly, Summer did value his opinion. He was a wise man. He would think of some way for Summer to save face and get out of the race.

"What do you mean, I better get in shape?" Summer stammered. She leaned against the workbench and decided to try again. "Grandpa, you don't understand! I want you to help me think of a way to get *out* of the race. Not get ready for it!"

Grandpa finally gave her his full attention. He placed his hammer on the table and sat on the edge of the chipped oak chair he was going to refinish someday. "What are you telling me, girl? That you're a quitter before you've even begun?"

"There isn't enough time," Summer argued. "And I'm not in shape for this, mentally or physically. I'm . . . puny."

"Nonsense, child. You've got the long legs, you're thin. . . . Why you're the spitting image of what a runner should be."

"But . . . but . . ."

"No buts about it. You've asked my advice, Summer. Now listen to me. You could do it. Now don't shake your head that way. You *could* do it. But you have to want it bad enough. And you have to work.

"Most important, you have to want it for you, not for David, not for me — not for anyone but yourself. I've never known you to be a quitter before, Summer. It's a trait the Irish don't abide."

"I've never tried anything like this before," Summer muttered. "I don't care if I win or not, I just don't want to look like a complete fool." There, the truth was out. Summer felt better just saying the words. She was always worried about what other people thought. Was that so terribly wrong? "Grandfather, I wish . . ."

"I'm waiting," her grandfather returned patiently.

"Maybe I could give it a try," Summer muttered with defeat.

"And I'll help you," he replied. "That's my girl. I knew you had your grandmother's spunk in you. It was just hidden under a few layers."

"Guess I better get started. Only problem

is, I don't know where to begin. I need new tennis shoes."

"You need a training program and a trainer. And you're in luck, little girl. You've got the best. Me!"

Humility was never one of Grandfather's strong points. Summer didn't quite hide her smile. "Then you really will help me?"

"Don't need to ask that. Of course I'll help you. We start tomorrow." Her grandfather rubbed his hands together and continued. "This afternoon we'll get you those shoes. I'll need a few things myself. We'll stop at the sporting goods store at the mall. Go and get your brother ready. I'll be up in a few minutes."

Summer had to admit that she hadn't seen her grandfather so excited about a project in a long time. He grinned in what she could only surmise was gleeful anticipation. He was already getting into the role of a trainer, she thought.

They had just walked into the house after their shopping jaunt when the phone rang. It was David.

"Just wondered what you were up to," David said in that husky voice that made Summer's stomach flip over.

"Helping with dinner," Summer answered. "What are you doing?"

"Nothing," David said. "I just got home and no one's here. They left a note about some cold chicken."

"We're having meatloaf. Not mine. Mom

made it," Summer giggled. "My last meat-loaf broke the garbage disposal."

"Sure sounds better than cold chicken. I hate cold chicken." Summer took the hint and asked David to hold on for a minute. She found her mother in the kitchen and asked her if David could join them for dinner.

"David, would you like to have dinner with us?" Summer asked in a breathless voice when she returned to the phone.

"Is it okay?"

"Of course. We would love to have you."

"Great," David answered.

"Fine," Summer said. "See you in about an hour?"

She didn't wait for his answer. She had to perform a miracle on her body and had less than sixty minutes in which to do it.


Grandpa's leprechauns were on Summer's side. Dinner was calm and orderly. In short, everyone behaved. David helped clear the table and then took Grandfather up on his offer to tour the basement.

Summer was amazed that she wasn't the least bit nervous about leaving David with her grandfather. Not since he had witnessed the runaway vacuum cleaner. Instinct told her that David understood and really cared about the elderly gentleman. It was a nice feeling, not being worried all the time.

After she finished the dishes, she joined Michael on the bottom step and watched while her grandfather showed David a few of his inventions. David seemed mesmerized by the vacuum cleaner and before long the two were busy taking the unit apart. David had entered Grandfather's world and it wasn't long before Summer realized he had forgotten she was even there. Jealousy reared its nasty head for a moment, but then Summer reminded herself that David was in *her* basement and that he was apparently having a good time.

Summer dragged a sleepy Michael off to bed, getting through his bath in record time with the promise that she would read some of the new *Jogging Manual* her grandfather had purchased today. It would be his bedtime story.

Michael was asleep within five minutes. The first chapter of the book could have put anyone to sleep, Summer decided. She moved back to the basement steps, book in hand, and began to read in earnest when she got to chapter five. That chapter was devoted to the marathon runner and kept mentioning *the wall* that each and every runner encountered at some point. It was an invisible wall, and the description of the body's reaction was vivid and depressing. Yet every runner that was quoted promised that once you got past the wall, a fresh spurt of energy mysteriously manufactured itself inside the body. It was all totally foreign to Summer and she wondered if David had ever experienced such a thing.

David and Grandfather stopped their work around nine-thirty and Summer suggested that she and David sit on the porch for a while. Summer fixed them each a glass of lemonade and they sat next to each other on the bright green glider, sipping their drinks.

David pulled her closer to him and took hold of her hand. "What are you thinking about?"

"The wall," Summer answered. "The runner's wall. Have you ever heard of it?"

"Sure," David replied. "Happens after the first ten or fifteen miles. You feel like you just ran smack into a cement wall."

"Have you? I mean, has it ever happened to you? Do you run that far?"

"I've never run more than eight miles a day and no, I've never experienced the wall. To tell you the truth, it kind of scares me."

"I've never experienced it either," Summer said, and almost laughed out loud with that admission. It was the understatement of the year.

"Where do you run? I've never seen you at the park."

"Oh, just around the neighborhood," Summer answered. It was getting harder and harder to look at him when she lied. She felt like she was about to grow a very long nose, just like in the fairy tale.

"You should try running in the park. It's exactly two miles to the gate and back, and the jogger's path is easy on your feet."

"When do you run?" Summer asked.

"After my morning lessons. My favorite time is around dinner, though. Before I eat of course. It's nice with the sun going down and all." David seemed a little uneasy with his admission.

"David, there's a bit of an artist's appreciation in you," Summer teased.

"Guess so," he answered with a grin. "If it's okay with you, I'm coming over tomorrow after dinner to help your grandfather. We think we've figured out what's wrong with the vacuum."

"Come for dinner," Summer suggested. She knew her mother wouldn't mind. Her parents might not understand how much Summer wanted to work at the Pizza Paddle with Regina, but they were more than generous with dinner invitations. Her friends were always welcome.

"If you're sure it's all right," David answered.

Summer nodded. "I better get going," David announced. He gave Summer a quick kiss and then stood up. Placing their glasses on the railing, he turned to her and pulled her into his arms. "Thanks for tonight," he said, hugging her. "I like being here."

What a nice thing to say, Summer thought. She felt herself blush and smiled. Try as she did, she couldn't seem to think of a suitable reply.

"How about going to bingo together Monday night? Think your grandfather would ride with me instead of walking?"

"I'm sure he would," Summer answered.

"I'll call you tomorrow." He leaned down and kissed her again, and Summer wrapped her arms around his waist, enthusiastically hugging him.

He gave her a sexy wink and started down the steps. "Good-night . . . Rosebud!" He chuckled all the way to the car.

She waited until the car pulled away before confronting her family. "Okay," she snapped like a drill sergeant when she found her grandfather and parents in the kitchen, "who told David my nickname was Rosebud?"

# $S^{ix}$

"I think I'm in love, Regina. Really, really in love." Summer was sitting on the edge of her bed, lacing her new tennis shoes while she spoke. Regina, sprawled across the middle of the bed, listened to Sumer's every word while she ate a chocolate chip cookie.

"How can you be sure? What are the symptoms?" Regina's tone indicated that she was serious. "I don't think I've ever been in love."

"When David and I are together, I get all . . ." Summer groped for the words to describe how she was feeling.

"What?"

"I can't explain it. Last night David ate dinner with us, and I inhaled a whole heap of beets before I remembered that I hated them. It's scary, Regina. All I can think about is David, what he's doing, what he's thinking. And when I'm with him, I feel so . . . complete. I'm not making sense, am I?"

"No," Regina answered. "But I think not making sense is all part of the package when you're in love. Do you think I'll ever fall in love?"

"Of course." Summer stood up and examined herself in the mirror. She was wearing a pair of faded cut-offs and a pink tank top. "I don't look like a runner, do I?"

"No, but I know what's missing," Regina replied. "You need a head band."

Summer laughed and immediately opened the top drawer of her bureau. Her hair was pulled back into a knot on the top of her head, and she carefully adjusted the pink sweatband into position. "Grandpa thought of everything." Summer said with a giggle. "I've got five of these, all different colors."

"Well, you look like a runner now. Come on, it's time to begin." Regina stated. "I'm going to ride my bike next to you and cheer you on."

It sounded so fun and so simple. Halfway around the park and Summer had a whole new appreciation for the runners of the world. They were all crazy!

"My side," Summer panted. "Regina, has my left side fallen off?"

"No. You're doing fine. Ignore the pain."

"That's easy for you to say, perched up there on your ten-speed. I'm dying and you tell me to ignore the pain. Sadist."

Summer ran a total of one and a half miles before her legs turned into rubber and she collapsed. Regina, bless her heart, didn't laugh. She helped Summer home but couldn't get her any further than the glider on the front porch.

"Now you're a real runner, Summer. You're all sweaty."

"If that was meant as a compliment you can forget it."

"How did it go, girls?" Grandpa's smiling face peeked around the screen door. Summer's groan brought a chuckle. He came to sit beside Summer and gently patted her hand. "Never said it would be easy, honey. How far did you get? The corner?"

"A mile and a half," Regina answered. "I kind of clocked her. She's real slow and her pace is sporadic, but it was a good start all the same, don't you think?"

"Mile and a half, you say?" Grandpa rubbed his chin. "Why, that's a mighty good start. Now you have to add a quarter of a mile every other day as I see it." He drummed his finger tips on the railing in an absentminded manner and then added, "Yep, quarter mile every other day and you'll be up to eight miles in no time."

It would take too much effort to yell and scream. The two of them were discussing her like she was a contender for the Kentucky Derby.

"No way," Summer muttered. "I'm going to be dead in a matter of minutes so don't make too many plans for me. The spirit is willing but the flesh is a mess."

"Going to get worse before it gets better, Summer," her grandfather predicted with a tinge of smugness. "Come morning and you'll be as stiff as your mother's ironing board. Got some liniment for you, and the sooner you get some of those aching muscles soothed, the better."

"Just like a horse," Summer said. "Except I don't feel like an expensive quarterhorse now. More like a swaybacked old nag."

"Go and soak in the tub," Regina suggested, "while your grandfather and I decide on your training schedule."

The hot bath water soothed Summer's screaming muscles, but nothing could calm her shattered thoughts. It was all so hopeless. Defeat enveloped her just like the bubbles in her bath, and salty tears began to roll down her cheeks.

She would lose David. Summer was sure of that. Not because she couldn't make it as a runner, but because she had lied to him. What kind of meaningful relationship could she hope for, based on deceit? It was too late to explain the entire situation to David. She had told too many fibs now. I've learned my lesson well, Summer thought. Never, never would she try to be something she wasn't. No matter what. Take me as I am, David Marshall, or not at all. Not at all! That was what was going to happen, as soon as David found out the truth. Summer visualized David's expression when he learned she had deceived him. She pictured Ann Logan telling him and that did the trick. "No way," she snapped. "Grandpa is right." Summer grimaced and gingerly lifted one leg high into the air. "Legs, you've won this battle, but I will win the war." It was a vow she would repeat again and again.

Morning brought a fresh wave of pain. Grandpa appeared at Summer's bedroom door with the first light of dawn and announced that it was time to get up.

"It's only six o'clock," Summer squealed when she was able to focus on the digital clock.

"Best time of day," her grandfather stated. "Now get dressed and meet me in the basement. I've got a little surprise for you."

It was useless to argue. It wasn't a bad dream; her grandfather was serious. The gray sweat suit he was wearing was ample testimony to that fact.

A brisk shower helped, but not much. Summer was in a foul mood when she stumbled down the basement steps.

The surprise turned out to be a new exercise mat placed in the center of the room. "This is where you can do your limbering-up exercises before you run. You can hurt yourself if you haven't stretched those muscles a bit. Can't start running right off."

Now he tells me, Summer thought.

"Look at the pictures in this exercise book. See? Now I want you to do these five exercises."

Summer knew better than to argue. Her grandfather was far more stubborn than she was, and had a temper that rivaled a number eight on the Richter scale early in the morning.

Better to get it over with. Summer forced herself not to gag when she opened the bottle of liniment her grandfather handed her, but the aroma was enough to knock her off her feet. She applied a liberal amount to her legs and then started the exercises. Her grandfather sat on his workbench, a stopwatch in his hand, and a whistle tied to a shoestring around his neck.

With each leg lift, Summer's mind screamed the words, I hate this. It might have been childish, but it did take her mind off her protesting muscles.

Twenty minutes later, Summer had to admit that she did feel a little more limber. Grandfather shouted words of encouragement when he pushed her out the front door. "Remember, at least one mile and a half today, and a tad more if you're up to it."

Summer didn't experience the wall that she had read about, but by the time she staggered into her house, she felt like she had been run over by a very large truck.

If only she could quit, or break a leg — anything to get out of this mess. The promise that it would get easier couldn't be believed. It had to be a myth. Anyone who actually enjoyed running just wasn't playing with a full deck. Except David, of course. He was the exception. Besides, everyone was allowed to have at least two faults, and David's were not so terribly bad. So what if he *liked* running and telling bad jokes? He was entitled.

# Seven

The next two weeks flew by. Each and every morning, no matter how late Summer went to bed, Grandfather appeared at her door at six sharp. Summer experienced a full range of reactions to the early morning ritual, from outright hatred to benign acceptance.

One morning it dawned on Summer that her grandfather was also making a sacrifice by getting up so early. And he always had a word of encouragement for her, no matter how grumpy she was. "Your cup is always half empty, Summer. Think of it in terms of being half full."

Summer thought about that old saying long and hard on her run. She was up to three and a half miles. She noticed that the awful pain in her side had finally disappeared, and that her pace seemed to even out.

Mrs. Hobard, the spry sixty-year-old jogger, was still passing Summer, but the gap was closing. The blue-haired lady had confided that she had been jogging for ten years and Summer had the advantage of youth on her side.

Another week passed and an even more amazing thing happened. Summer, though she would die before she admitted it to her family, was actually beginning to enjoy her runs. Feelings of well-being and confidence were growing inside her. It was as if she was becoming in tune with her body, pushing it to a healthy limit.

In fact, Summer's entire outlook began to change. The time spent running became Summer's special time. She no longer thought about the discomfort, but concentrated on the issues that were bothering her. Her views began to change, too. She started seeing her family not as a zoo but as loving individuals. The conclusion that she was part of a very special family began to make a little sense. They would still embarrass her at times, but that thought didn't bring chills to her insides like it used to.

One morning a boy by the name of Luke paced alongside Summer and chatted with her for a few minutes. She had noticed him a couple of times before, but thought that he was older . . . too old for Regina. When he mentioned that he was a transfer student and would be a senior next year at her high school, Summer's radar picked up. Not only was Luke a nice-looking boy, but he also fit the most important requirement. He was tall. Summer would do a good turn for her friend and introduce her to Luke, and she would enjoy a little friendly revenge on Carl Benson at the same time. How sweet it will be, Summer thought as she raced home.

"What do you mean I have to start running? Are you sick or something?" Regina's screech was loud and clear over the phone. Summer forced the laughter out of her voice and let Regina rant and rave a good five minutes before she interrupted with *vital* information.

"We're talking blond hair, dreamy brown eyes with little gold chips in them, deep sexy voice, nice personality, and, last but not least, exceptionally tall. I rest my case."

"Will you go shopping with me?"

"What for?"

"A new jogging outfit, of course."

"Certainly." Summer giggled. "And Regina, because I'm such a good friend, I'll even let you borrow my special liniment."

It was decided that Regina would spend the night so that Summer could get her up in the morning. Summer set the alarm for five-thirty, correctly assuming that Regina would reed a good half hour to wake up and get with it.

Summer had showered, dressed, and finished her warm-up exercises the next morning before Regina appeared at the kitchen doorway.

"I'm warning you, Summer, this guy better

be worth it. *I'm* talking a cross between Mr. America and Superman — or better."

"He is, he is," Summer replied. "You look super, Regina, even if your eyes are only half opened."

"Let's eat and plan our strategy."

"No," Summer replied, "you shouldn't run on a full stomach. Now let's get going. We don't want to miss Luke."

"Okay. I'll meet you in the garage," Regina said, turning.

"Why the garage?"

"To get our bikes, dummy."

"Regina! The park is only a block away. We are going to run to the park. Got that?"

"What? And get all sweaty before I even meet him?"

"If you don't work up a sweat, he'll know you aren't serious about running. All runners take it seriously, Regina. Trust me on this. Sweat is a definite asset."

"Are you making fun of me?" Regina accused in a tight voice.

"Of course not," Summer protested. "Now come on."

On the way to the park, Regina brought up the subject of David. "Is he still coming over every night?" Envy laced her question, bringing a smile to Summer's face. She dearly loved to talk about David.

"He's coming over this afternoon. Says he has a job for both of us and wants to tell me about it."

"Think your parents will let you come to the Pizza Paddle with me and Gregg tonight?"

"Can't. Grandpa is having poker tonight and Mom and Dad are going over to the Scanlons'."

"Okay."

Summer heard the rejection in Regina's voice and immediately felt a little guilty. "But tomorrow night I can go with you."

"Good," Regina said. "I'll just switch it to tomorrow then. If this Luke is as good as you say, and he goes absolutely crazy for me, then we can double-date, okay?"

Summer smiled and nodded her head. Regina certainly did like to plan ahead.

They reached the entrance to the park and Regina whispered, "Be sure and nudge me when you get a glance at Luke."

"Regina, you won't be able to miss him. He's the only giant in the park."

A short time later, Luke appeared. Summer and Regina had just begun their run, so Regina gave a fairly good showing. She almost looked like a pro. Almost.

Summer introduced the two to each other and Luke did seem more than politely interested in Regina. At least that was what Summer and Regina decided after he had waved good-bye and yelled, "See you both tomorrow."

"This means I'm committed, right?" Regina groaned.

"Is he worth it?"

"Oh, Summer, the things we do for love. Of course he's worth it."

"Can I say I told you so?" Summer asked with a great show of smugness.

"Only if you want a fat lip," Regina predicted.

"Okay. Look, now that Luke is gone, why don't you take it easy and just jog around the park at a slow pace while I do my four miles."

"I will, Summer. You go on."

The run was exhilarating. When Summer finished, she was extremely proud of herself. She had made five miles today instead of her estimated four, and felt wonderfully exhausted.

David remembered that Michael had been invited to a birthday party and that Summer would be on her own for a few hours. He surprised her with a picnic lunch. Summer was thrilled.

She didn't have time to get all worked up over the outing or agonize about what she should wear. She opened the screen door in her uniform, cut-off jeans and tank top, but David didn't mind at all.

"Give me a couple of minutes to change," she suggested.

"You look great," David replied. "Just grab some shoes and let's go. What time do you have to be back?"

"Michael will be home at two," Summer told him.

"That gives us a little over two hours,"

David announced, glancing down at his watch. "Your grandfather want to come along?"

Summer smiled. David was so thoughtful. "He went over to Mr. Clancy's house," Summer explained. "We should be back before he comes home, but I'll leave him a note just in case."

Five minutes later, David and Summer were in his car and on their way. They decided to have their picnic in the park and found a nice, secluded spot far enough away from the swimming pool and the crowd.

David had gone to a lot of trouble, and prepared all the food himself. Somehow, the peanut butter and grape jelly sandwiches tasted absolutely wonderful, probably because David had made them.

"Peanut butter isn't gourmet, but it's loaded with protein," David advised Summer between bites.

"I love peanut butter," Summer told him. She finished her second sandwich and stretched out on the blanket David had thought to bring along. Propped up by her elbows, she lazily crossed her ankles and smiled. "This is fun, David. Very spontaneous!"

"You like spontaneous?" David asked with a mysterious twinkle in his eyes. When Summer nodded, he leaned down and kissed her. He tasted like peanut butter and smelled like spice.

"I think I love spontaneous," Summer

whispered when the kiss ended.

David smiled at her, a tender, full-of-caring smile, Summer decided. He sat back up then, and folded his long legs Indian style. "I've got something to show you," David said. He started hunting through the large grocery sack and Summer noticed a little blush creep up his neck. Her curiosity was caught.

David pulled out a small notebook from the bottom of the sack and then looked over at Summer. "Promise you won't laugh?" he asked a little hesitantly. Before she could answer him, he shook his head. "That was a stupid question. I know you won't laugh."

He opened the notebook, closed it again, and handed it to Summer. She sat up, holding the notebook and watching David. He was acting very busy, putting napkins and sandwich bags in the sack. He was nervous, which made Summer want to hug him.

Very slowly she opened the notebook, smiling when she saw the beautiful sketch of a unicorn. It was done in pencil, and it was very, very good. "This is wonderful," Summer said, almost in awe. She didn't look up at David. Very carefully, she wiped her hands on her cut-offs and turned the page. A lioness, with three cubs nestled around her, filled the page. It was as good as the unicorn, Summer thought, if not better. Without saying another word, Summer continued to look through the book, both amazed and mesmerized by the drawings.

"Do you have any idea how talented you

are?" she asked when she closed the book.

"You really think so?" David asked. He looked a little embarrassed and vulnerable, too.

"David, these are good!" Summer stated with great emphasis. "You have to know that. Have you shown them to anyone?"

"Just you," David said. He smiled, and Summer was reminded of a rainbow after a spring rain. "'I'm glad you like them."

"Like them! I love them," Summer replied. She opened the notebook again and said, "I think the unicorn is my favorite. They're all good," she rushed on, "but unicorns are kind of . . . mystical and romantic."

"I think so, too," David said.

"When did you learn to do this?" Summer asked.

David shrugged and said, "I just sort of picked it up."

"Haven't you taken any art classes?" Summer inquired.

"No, but next semester I'm going to," David explained. "You really like them, don't you?" He was wearing a grin from ear to ear, and Summer smiled.

"You know I do," Summer told him. "How come you haven't shown these to me before?"

"I felt kind of funny about it, I guess," David admitted. "I mean, I was afraid you wouldn't like them, or. . . ."

Summer was shaking her head with exasperation. "I like them a lot, David. You have talent."

"I'm glad you feel that way," David said.

"How come there aren't any people sketches?" Summer asked. "I mean, the animals are wonderful but I think you should branch out."

"I've never wanted to draw people, until now," David said. "How about if I try to sketch you."

"Really?" Summer was brushing her hair back over her shoulders and sitting a little straighter. "Now?"

"No," David said, laughing. "I didn't bring my pencils," he explained. "I'm glad you think it's neat. My dad doesn't say anything but he would rather I played football all day. He's kind of hung up on being macho, I guess."

"Parents can have strange ideas, David," Summer said in a gentle voice. "I bet someday you'll be rich and famous."

"I want to have my own comic strip," David blurted out. "Do my own drawings and everything."

Summer laughed. "So that's why you tell jokes?" she asked. "To get in practice?"

"Yeah, I guess so," David admitted.

"I've got to tell you the truth, David," Summer said, grinning. "Your jokes aren't so hot, but your drawings are dynamic."

"You just haven't heard my really good jokes," David protested. He then proceeded to tell her at least five pretty awful jokes, and didn't seem to mind that she wasn't laughing along with him after the punch lines were delivered.

"Like I said, David, your drawings are great. Now, the jokes. . . ."

"That's why I like you so much, Summer. You're always honest with me. I can count on you. The last girl I dated really turned me off on girls in general," David said, growing serious.

"Why?" Summer asked, frowning.

"She told me she wanted to be my girl and didn't want me to date anyone else. I was glad. . . . I mean, I really liked her and I was quick to agree. Then I find out she'd said the same thing to two other guys. She had her own little club going."

"I would never lie about *that*," Summer said. "Sometimes I exaggerate a little bit, but everyone does." She lifted her shoulders and couldn't look at David, thinking of her lie about running. Maybe that wasn't a lie, she considered.

David looked at his watch and frowned. "Much as I hate to, I better take you home. Superman will be finished with his party soon."

Summer helped David fold the blanket. They held hands on the way to the car, stopping several times for quick kisses and long smiles.

# $E^{ight}$

The next afternoon Summer met Regina and Gregg at the Pizza Paddle. She wished with all her heart that it would start raining so that David wouldn't have to work, and he could join them.

The Pizza Paddle was crowded and the aroma of pepperoni and spicy Italian sausage reminded Summer of just how hungry she was. She sat down between Gregg and Regina and the three of them devoured an extra-large pizza in record time. Summer was just finishing her Coke when Regina whispered in a furious voice. "Don't look up."

The temptation was too great. The look on Regina's face alerted Summer that something was terribly wrong, and she promptly ignored her advice and quickly turned toward the door. All color drained from her face. There, standing in the doorway, was David. And he wasn't alone. Ann Logan was right beside him, her bright red fingernails resembling tentacles of ownership cemented to David's arm.

"What are you going to do?" Regina's question brought Summer's confused gaze back to her. She tried to smile.

"I don't know. Try to act natural, I guess. Got any better ideas?"

"What's going on?" mumbled Gregg, his mouth full of pizza.

"Summer's boyfriend just walked in with Ann Logan. Don't look," Regina demanded. To Summer she added, "He hasn't spotted you yet. Want to make a dash for the back door?"

"Absolutely not. If David prefers Ann's company, then so be it. It doesn't make sense, though. He said he had to work! And I thought I was his girl friend. I guess I was wrong. I mean, he never said we weren't supposed to see anyone else, but I thought . . . after he showed me his drawings — "

"Summer, you're rambling and muttering," Regina interrupted.

"I don't care," Summer whispered. She said the words with a negligent shrug. Inside, she felt like she was dying. She prayed that she wouldn't burst into tears and took a deep breath to gain some control.

"I've got an idea," Regina said. "Gregg, put your arm around the back of Summer's chair."

"Why?" Gregg wanted to know.

"Just do it," Regina ordered. "If Ann is

David's date, then you're Summer's date, got that?"

"What?" Now it was Summer who wanted to know what was going on.

"If David is with Ann, then you're with Gregg. Gregg, act like you're crazy for Summer. And don't argue. You still owe me twenty dollars, remember?"

"Does this cancel the debt?"

"Yes. Now do it. Summer, move closer."

"Look, we should find out if David has a date with Ann before we — "

"Open your eyes, Summer. That much is obvious," Regina explained. "All boys are slime."

"Here they come," Gregg said. "Give me your hand, Summer."

"What?" Summer was so miserable she just wanted to crawl into the nearest hole.

"Hi, Summer!" David's voice sounded so cheerful, and that confused Summer even more.

"Hi, everyone!" The high-pitched voice of delight sounded just like a fingernail sliding down a chalkboard to Summer's ears.

"Hello, David. Hi, Ann." Her voice sounded flat and totally devoid of any emotion, but it was the best Summer could do.

David couldn't seem to look directly at her. He kept his eyes focused on Gregg's arm around Summer's shoulders. And he suddenly seemed very embarrassed. His face got all red and blotchy.

Why oh why did it have to be Ann Logan?

Summer wailed to herself. It proved that David was no better than all the other stupid males in the city. He, too, had fallen under Ann's spell. The baser side of Summer wanted to yell and scream at the injustice of it all, or at the very least growl a little, but she decided to present the picture of serene dignity.

Introductions were made and Gregg suggested that David and Ann join them. David seemed a little reluctant but finally pulled up two chairs and sat down right across from Summer and Gregg. Regina played the hostess at the head of the table.

"David's been telling me the funniest jokes on the way over here," Ann giggled.

"Let's order another pizza," Gregg suggested. "I'm still hungry."

"Why don't we get a jumbo and all split it?" David suggested. "Everyone like anchovies?"

"I hate them. They make me gag," Summer said before she could stop herself.

"Oh, I just love them," Ann interjected.

David leaned toward Summer. "I called you and your mom said you were here, so I. . . . She didn't tell me you had a date," he added in a halting voice.

Gregg had just taken hold of Summer's hand and she tried to pull away. Gregg was having none of it. A tug of war was the result and Summer lost. She gave Regina a look that demanded help, but Regina was talking to Ann and didn't notice.

She continued to pull, and snapped at David, "But you had one anyway so what's the difference?"

David looked so hurt that Summer felt like crying, until Ann returned her attention to her date. Then she got good and mad! Why should she feel guilty when he was the one with the actual date? "I didn't know you were dating Ann," Summer said as soon as Regina dragged Ann over to the jukebox.

"Sort of," David hedged, staring at Gregg's death grip on Summer's hand. "Ann's father needs help with the run. He asked me to head the publicity part. It's an important job and I've already got it all figured out. Ann and I think we should make at least thirty posters and distribute them all over town. Mr. Logan showed me the T-shirts they're going to sell and they're really neat. Since all the money goes to charity, maybe the banks will help us out and put some on display. Ann thought it would be a good idea to sell them at the grocery stores, too. You know, set up a card table outside with a big sign and. . . ." His voice trailed off and he gave Summer a shrug.

"Would you like me to help?" Summer couldn't keep the eagerness out of her voice.

"If you're not too busy," he replied. "I thought we could use your dining room table . . . it's so big, and we could do the posters there." David went on to explain his strategy and Summer began to feel a little better. Gregg finally let go of her and she was able to lean forward, her chin resting on her hand, while she listened with what she hoped was rapt attention.

The feeling that things weren't so bad didn't last long. Ann came back to the table and scooted her chair closer to David and proceeded to have a whispered conversation with him.

Summer began to feel quite desperate. She nudged Gregg and whispered, "Talk to David about something," she demanded.

Gregg still had one arm draped around Summer's chair. "If anyone sees me with you, I'll leave town," he whispered in her ear.

"Thanks Gregg. I'm crazy about you, too," Summer snapped. She couldn't look at him. Her eyes were glued to David, watching the way he smiled at Ann. She couldn't remember him ever smiling at her *that* way! Ann took hold of David's hand and Summer was quick to notice that David didn't seem to mind.

The pizza arrived but Summer didn't eat any. Her stomach was too upset. She didn't have the heart to join in the conversation and was almost relieved when Gregg said, "Think we could leave now? One of my friends might walk in."

"You really know how to flatter a girl," Summer muttered. In a louder voice she said, "David, why don't you bring the posters over tomorrow afternoon and we'll get started."

Regina stayed at the Pizza Paddle, helping her father, and Gregg and Summer walked out together. Gregg was nice enough to keep his mouth shut while he drove her home and Summer was able to make it to her room before she started to cry.

David didn't call the next morning but appeared at her front door instead, his arms loaded down with posterboard and magic markers. Michael was busy playing at the neighbors and Grandpa had gone to the shopping center.

The two of them were all alone in the house and it was the perfect time to clear the air. The problem was that David was being so cool and aloof.

"David, when we're finished with the posters I'd like to really talk to you about something," Summer finally said.

David frowned and then nodded. "Gregg?"

"And Ann," Summer added. "Okay?"

"Okay," David replied. He smiled his first real smile and Summer beamed in return.

The screen door opened and Grandpa walked in, loaded down with packages he immediately carried to his room. Summer was disappointed. She didn't want to talk to David in front of her grandfather and decided to hurry and resolve the problem immediately. "What did you mean by a 'sort of' date?" she asked, pretending great concentration on the poster board in front of her.

The phone rang before David could reply. He answered it and called to her grandfather. Summer stood up and stretched, accepting that she would have to wait until after lunch to have her little talk with David. She left David sitting at the table and went into the kitchen to prepare lunch. Once Grandpa had eaten, he would probably take his nap. The sooner the meal was done, the better.

Summer pushed the swinging door that connected the dining room with the kitchen and asked David to clear a spot on the table.

The next time she hurried into the room, she overheard her grandfather. He was bragging on the phone about her, making outrageous statements about what a fast runner she was, and Summer had to smile. Grandpa dearly loved to brag!

David looked up at Summer and winked, and she knew that he, too, was listening to her grandfather's conversation.

Summer wasn't gone more than five minutes, but the next time she came into the dining room, David looked at her with a frown on his face. He seemed puzzled, Summer thought. Puzzled and irritated.

Summer returned to the kitchen for the pitcher of lemonade but she could hear David talking to her grandfather. She paused and felt the blood drain from her face when she heard her grandfather explain how she had just started running.

Michael came skipping in the back door then, full of chatter. "Summer, I've got a rock. . . ."

"Not now, Michael," Summer snapped. Her mind was racing with excuses *if* David realized that she had lied to him. The door swung open and David stood there, glaring at Summer.

"Hi, David," Michael said. "I've got a rock."

"Hi, Mike. Summer, your grandfather just told me that you've only been running for about a month." David sounded surprised.

"Oh, you know how Grandpa likes to exaggerate," Summer replied, trying to sound blasé. "David, will you take this pitcher into the dining room. I'll get the chips."

"He says you started running after Ann Logan's party, that Regina talked you into it."

"Michael, go and wash your hands," Summer stammered. "David, what's the big deal about when I started to run?"

"The big deal? If it's true, you lied to me," David stated.

Summer acted disgusted and marched by David. She put the pitcher on the table and turned around, knowing that David was right behind her. She was stalling, trying to come up with a logical explanation that would appease David and not make her grandfather sound like he had made the whole thing up.

"Summer, you know how important it is to me that we never, ever lie to each other. How can we build a good relationship if we can't trust each other?" David looked hurt.

"David, you're getting all upset over nothing," Summer soothed.

"Just answer one question, Summer,"

David demanded. "Did you or did you not lie to me?"

"Not exactly," Summer stated.

"What does not exactly mean?" David asked sarcastically.

What was the use? Summer asked herself. She might as well admit the truth. "Oh, all right! Yes, I did lie, David. But it was a little, insignificant exaggeration, not an outright whopper," she explained.

"Then it's true? You really only started running after Ann's party?" He sounded incredulous.

What did he want, blood? Summer asked herself. Honestly, he was being so self-righteous! Didn't he ever tell a fib?

"Look, Summer, just tell me why? I want to understand," David said. His voice was softer now.

How could she explain? She would die before she admitted that the entire reason was Ann Logan. He was dating her now, wasn't he? How could he possibly understand?

Summer shook her head. No, she couldn't tell him. He would never, ever understand. Boys weren't jealous like girls were — or were they?

"So what else have you lied to me about?"

The quietly stated question infuriated Summer. She turned around with fire in her eyes. "Nothing! Now it's up to you to decide if you believe me or not," she stated.

"Ha!" David snorted.

It was the snort that did it. Summer fairly exploded.

"What's that supposed to mean?" she yelled. "Look, I could have lied and told you that I loved your jokes, but I didn't. And the anchovies," she suddenly remembered. "I could have said I loved them!" She ran out of the kitchen and into the dining room.

David was right on her heels. "Oh yeah? Well some people love my jokes. Ann Logan appreciates them," he added in a loud voice.

Summer felt like she had just been stabbed. "And you believe her?"

"Sure," David said. "*She's* an honest person."

"Anyone who laughs at your stupid jokes is not being honest," Summer replied.

"So why didn't you tell me you had a date with Gregg?" David suddenly switched topics.

Summer countered his question with one of her own. "Why didn't you tell me you had a date with Ann?"

"We don't have an agreement or anything," David muttered. "I mean, if you want to date other boys, it's fine with me."

"I didn't have a date with Gregg," Summer said. There, the truth was out.

David didn't believe her. "Ha! Ann told me you were seeing Gregg. I didn't believe her until last night. I didn't think you'd lie about something like — "

"If you say 'ha' one more time, I'm going to scream," Summer interrupted.

"You two having a difference of opinion?" Grandpa's voice intruded on the heated argument and both Summer and David blushed.

"And when I asked you if you wanted to run with me," David continued, "I seem to remember that you said you liked to jog by yourself early in the morning so you could think things over," David muttered in a clipped voice.

"What are you, a memory bank?" Summer snapped out. She folded her arms and glared at him.

David was almost out the door when she called out, "I guess you're going over to Ann's house."

"Maybe," David called back.

"The perfect couple," Summer muttered under her breath.

She couldn't look at her grandfather, still too angry that he had accidentally told David about her exaggeration. Instead, she lifted Michael and put him in his chair. She shoved a sandwich in front of him and said, "Eat!"

Two hours later a phone call to Regina didn't make Summer feel any better. When she'd told her friend about the argument with David, Regina had said, "Couldn't you have lied your way out of it?"

Summer was too miserable to argue or defend herself. She was sick of lies. And sick of holding back the tears, too. She went up to her room right after dinner and cried until there weren't any tears left. The release didn't make her feel any better and Summer punched her pillow to vent some of her anger and frustration. The anger slowly receded, but in its stead, loneliness, aching and desolate, filled the void.

Snuggled in her blankets, she fell asleep with the thought that she wouldn't have to get up at six tomorrow morning. Who wanted to run in a dumb race, anyway?

# Nine

Grandfather was having none of it! "What do you mean you're not going to run today?" His indignant bellow threatened to wake the entire household.

"I've decided I don't want to be a runner," Summer muttered into the pillow. She stared at the tiny pink flower pattern on her sheets rather than look at her grandfather. She was afraid she would see his disappointment and she wasn't up to coping with that this early in the morning. She just wanted to be left alone, to wallow in her misery.

"You've invested too much to quit now. I won't have it! Do you hear me? Take those covers off your ears, girl, and listen to me. I don't know what's got your feathers ruffled, but you can tell me all about it while you do your warm-up exercises. I'm giving you just ten minutes to get down to the basement."

Well, she wasn't going to say anything to

him! He wouldn't understand anyway. No one would. Not even Regina. Hadn't Regina admitted that she, herself, had never really been in love? She was lucky, Summer decided. Loving someone was the pits.

"What is the matter with you?" her grandfather asked. "Your legs cramping up on you again?" He seemed very concerned and Summer almost squealed her frustration when she saw him reach for the ever-ready bottle of liniment.

"I'm okay," she snapped. "I just don't feel like running today."

"Can't miss a single day. You're on a schedule, remember?"

"Grandpa, I want to quit. Can't you understand that?"

"I won't hear of it. You're just out of sorts today. Now, tell me why." It wasn't a suggestion but a demand, and his large bulk was blocking her only escape, the stairs. It didn't look like she would be going anywhere until she talked to him.

"I saw David with Ann yesterday afternoon. He's dating her regularly now, I just know it! And it's all your fault, Grandpa!" She was busy doing her twenty sit-ups and gasped with each word. "If it was anyone else in the whole world I don't think I'd care as much. But Ann Logan. . . ."

"How is all this my fault?"

"You told David the truth and I lied to him. If you hadn't said anything — "

"If you hadn't lied," her grandfather interrupted. "That's the heart of it, isn't it now?"

"Okay, okay, so I lied. I can't stand Ann Logan. She's always telling lies and it hasn't hurt her any. And she always takes my boyfriends away," she lied.

"Jealous," her grandfather replied in a tone that suggested more than a little disgust. "You're entirely too young to get serious over a boy, young lady. Plenty of time for that later on."

She knew he wouldn't understand and rolled her eyes heavenward in irritation. "Well, I don't own him, that's for sure. But I thought he liked being with me. Guess I was wrong. I'm just a lying, boring person," she added. She was feeling extremely sorry for herself — and she didn't mind one bit.

"Nonsense! Of course David likes being with you. You've just disappointed him. He'll come around," her grandfather insisted. He seemed exasperated with the entire conversation, Summer decided, but she didn't care.

"No, he doesn't. If he did, he wouldn't have gotten all upset over such a stupid, little thing. He's not very understanding now that I think about it. . . ."

Suddenly Summer wanted to run, to make herself go the limit. To make herself hurt as much on the outside as she was hurting on the inside. Maybe she would just keel over from exhaustion, and the ache deep inside would stop. It was certainly worth a try. At least she would be able to get away from her grandfather and his lecture! "I'm going to run after all."

"Never doubted it," her grandfather answered with a grin. "Work off some of that self-pity. Jealousy is a destructive emotion, Summer. Get rid of it."

Those words kept repeating themselves inside her head as she raced around the circular path that edged the park. She passed the regulars and literally sailed by the jogging Luke. Summer became obsessed with going faster and faster. The pain in her side registered a brief complaint and then subsided. Summer ignored it, her fellow runners, and the beautiful scenery, concentrating with all her might on catching the wind and finding sweet numbness from her pain.

"You taking some new vitamins, Summer?" Luke asked when he caught up with her. They were running side by side, Summer quite effortlessly, while Luke pushed and panted.

"No," Summer answered. "Just trying to work off a little hostility."

"You're fast. Ever been timed?" Luke asked when they stopped to rest.

"Not really," Summer replied. "My grandfather clocked me when I first started but I was really slow then."

"Boy, you're darn fast now. How long you been running?" There was admiration in his voice and a tinge of pride crept into Summer's spine.

"Just since the start of vacation," she answered.

"You're kidding!" Luke shook his head and laughed. "You're crazy if you don't go out for track next year. I think you could set new records."

Summer wasn't sure what he meant by that but she really wasn't interested. "Are you entered in the Regis Run, Luke?"

"Yes, what about you?"

"I'm supposed to run, but I don't know if I will."

"You're out of your mind if you don't, Summer. I've never seen a girl run that fast," he praised her. "You ought to go for it. You could win. Honest."

"Such optimism." Summer chuckled. "You sound just like my grandfather. I've never run in a race before, and I don't know how fast everyone else will be. They might all leave me at the starting gate. I just don't . . ."

Summer could feel herself blushing and closed her eyes. She felt vulnerable but not at all humble. The conflicting emotions were confusing.

"You don't what?" Luke asked.

"I don't want to make a fool of myself and come in last."

"Last? Not a chance," Luke responded. Amazement laced his words and Summer opened her eyes and looked at him. He *was* serious. "I don't think you have any idea how good you are, but take my word for it. Boy, are you going to surprise some people."

Now Summer's interest was really piqued. "What do you mean?" She was suddenly all ears.

"There's always a group that enters all the cash races and they take the top prizes. I call them the pros. And you're just like a dark horse, so to speak. No one has ever heard of you. You're going to knock them for a loop. Reminds me of the story about President Truman. He was called a dark horse and the newspapers were so sure he was going to lose that they all printed the other guy's name — Dewey I think — and then Truman won. He surprised a lot of people, and I'm betting you will, too."

"You really think so, Luke? You're not just saying that to be nice?" She didn't even listen to his response, for her mind was filled with pictures of David and Ann, and the looks of astonishment on their faces if she did finish in the top ten. Excitement surged through her. Was it just wishful thinking, or was there really a chance?

"It's in the bag, Summer. Look, tomorrow I'll bring a stopwatch and time you. Then you'll believe me."

"Sounds good to me," Summer replied with a grin.

"Hey, I'm starved. Let's go get some donuts and work on your strategy."

Luke was like a healing balm to her injured pride. There wasn't any physical attraction between the two of them, Summer admitted, but he was so easy to talk to. Of course, she couldn't tell him about David. But it felt good to have someone take such an interest in her. The ache of losing David was still terribly fresh, just like a raw wound, Summer analyzed on her way home, but the bleeding wasn't nearly as bad. She would never be the same, she realized with a little self-pity, but she would survive. And just as important, she would show them! She would win the race or die trying. That grim thought spiraled into pictures of David kneeling before her casket, weeping and begging for forgiveness.

"And I thought you were my best friend!" The accusation was issued in a high-pitched voice. Regina, hands on her hips, stood on Summer's front porch, glaring her anger.

Summer was in no mood for guessing games. She didn't have the faintest idea what Regina was blustering about. Her head throbbed from Michael's constant chatter, and from the trauma of thinking about David and Ann being together.

"Come on into the kitchen," Summer invited. "I've got to set the table for dinner."

"I'll help, you traitor," Regina muttered, following behind Summer.

"What are you talking about?"

"Luke," Regina announced. "That's who I'm talking about."

"What about him?" Summer asked. "Why am I a traitor?"

"Have a nice breakfast date?" Regina asked sarcastically.

"Regina, give me a break. Today has been the pits. Just tell me what you're talking about."

"Did you or did you not go out with Luke this morning?" Now Regina sounded hurt, and Summer finally gave her her full attention.

"Who told you I had a date with Luke?" Summer would have laughed then, or at the very least snorted, but the expression on Regina's face suggested she better not.

"Gregg saw you," Regina defended. "And when he described the guy you were with, I knew it was Luke. David doesn't have blond hair."

"Oh, for heaven's sake. Luke and I just walked over to the donut shop after we ran today. *And*," Summer continued, "we talked about you some of the time. Where were you, by the way? You were supposed to run today, remember?"

"I know, but I forgot to set my alarm clock," Regina answered. "You really talked about me?" she asked. She wore a sheepish expression and Summer smiled. "What did he say? Tell me everything. Don't leave out a single word."

"He thinks you're cute," Summer told her, "and I think he's getting ready to ask you out. He wanted to know if you were seeing anyone special or going steady."

Regina had a hard time containing her enthusiasm. "Then you really didn't have an actual, for-real date at all. I knew you really didn't," Regina continued. "I didn't *actually* believe Gregg at all."

"I hate all boys," Summer stated. "They cause nothing but pain and aggravation."

"I don't think it's the boys," Regina said. "It's boys in combination with Ann Logan. If Luke does ask me out, I'm going to keep him clear of Ann's clutches. But what about you? Have you figured out a way to get David back?"

"I don't want him back," Summer lied. "And I don't want to talk about it anymore. It's too depressing. Let's run away and join a convent."

"Don't be silly, Summer," Regina chided. "You'd look terrible in black. If Luke doesn't ask me out soon, I'm hanging up my tennis shoes. Tomorrow will be his last chance."

"Want to spend the night so I can get you up in the morning? And by the way, I think you should be the first to know, since you are my best friend. I've decided that I'm going to win that bloody race!"

Getting Regina up and at 'em proved to be a real battle. Summer had to be quite ruthless and at one point felt like an army sergeant. "Come on, time to get up," she said for the tenth time. "Luke's waiting for you," she added in a singsong voice.

That did the trick. Regina staggered out of

bed and planted herself in the center of the bedroom, blinking in confusion. She looked quite pathetic but Summer continued to be heartless. After all, it was all for Regina's love life. She grabbed Regina by the shoulders and propelled her into the bathroom, and left her hanging over the sink, muttering. "Meet me in the basement in five minutes, no later," Summer told her.

By the time Summer had dragged Regina at a snail's pace to the park, she was decidedly disgusted. She wished she hadn't invited Regina to run with her and she was a little ashamed that she felt that way. Regina was her best friend, she reminded herself, and feeling irritated with her was somewhat of a betrayal, wasn't it?

Besides, Regina had stayed up half the night listening to Summer rehash her hurts over David.

Summer took her frustration and guilt out on her run, leaving Regina by the pool as she raced into the beckoning wind. The simple truth was that Regina just didn't understand what had happened to Summer. How could she? Summer barely understood, herself. She just knew that this wasn't a whim any longer. No, it had become compulsive. Running each day had become as necessary as her father's second cup of coffee — and just as addictive. Summer was hard pressed to explain it; she just knew that she felt better and more alive than ever when she was running. And with all the misery in her life right now, she decided she needed all the edges she could get.

Summer passed Regina and was pleased to see Luke standing beside her. Luke yelled hello and held the stopwatch up, indicating that he had begun to time her.

When she finished her run, Luke read off her time in an excited voice. She didn't know what the numbers meant but assumed she had done a good job. Luke asked both Summer and Regina to go for donuts but Summer declined, knowing that Regina would want to be alone with Luke.

# Ten

An entire two weeks passed without a word from David. Summer kept herself busy, running sometimes twice a day to fill the time, and feeling absolutely miserable inside. She vacillated between outright misery and anger. Every time she thought about David dating Ann, she was miserable; every time she thought how stubborn and unforgiving David was turning out to be, she was angry.

Early one afternoon, when Summer returned from swimming at Regina's house, her mother met her on the front steps. One look at the bleak expression in her eyes told Summer some trauma was about to unfold.

"What did Michael do now?"

"I've lost your grandfather."

Now a normal person would have at least blinked with that bit of news, but not Summer. It had happened before, and in probability, it would happen again.

"When did you last see him?" Summer asked. She was already walking towards the garage, to get her bike.

"It's that new medicine he started taking last week," her mother said. "It makes him a little confused." It was an excuse.

"Mom, Grandpa hasn't been confused in a long, long time. I think he just went on an errand or something. Don't worry."

Summer searched the neighborhood, stopping to ask children and adults if they had seen her grandfather pass by. Everyone knew him, but no one had seen him today.

She was about to give up her search when one of the gas station attendants said he had seen her grandfather just a few minutes ago. Summer hurried off in the direction he gave. She spotted her grandfather through the tinted glass of the ice-cream store but almost fell off her bike when she noticed who he was sitting next to. David! David — and Ann Logan.

"What a mess," Summer muttered. She became angry with herself when she felt her hands begin to tremble.

Plastering a smile on her face, she entered the shop and went directly over to her grandfather. "Mom's looking for you," she stated a bit briskly.

She only looked at her grandfather, concentrated on his face in her bid to completely ignore David and Ann. It was rude, but Summer didn't care.

A part of her brain registered the fact that

her grandfather seemed completely aware of where he was and what he was doing. His expression didn't look the least bit confused.

"Why would your mother be looking for me?" He didn't appear to want an answer as he dug into his pocket for some change. "David, nice to see you again. Come by the house sometime and I'll show you my latest invention. I miss your visits."

So do I, Summer wanted to say. But of course she didn't and couldn't, not with Ann hanging all over him. Ann wore a smile of the contented, a smile of the victorious. She knows how miserable I am, and she's relishing it, Summer thought.

"Nice to see you again, David, Ann." Summer finally spoke, pleased that her voice sounded just right, not too brisk at all. She still couldn't look into David's eyes, but she got close, staring at his shirt collar while she spoke.

Grandfather was ready to leave, and without a backward glance, Summer followed him out the door.

"Mom didn't know where you were. She got worried," Summer said. She walked beside her grandfather, pushing the bicycle between them.

"Just doing a few errands. I left her a note," Grandfather replied. "No need for her to get upset."

"You know Mom," Summer answered. "She likes to get uptight. Keeps her slim and trim."

Grandfather laughed at Summer's astute description.

"Did you sit down with David and Ann? Or did they come in and sit down with you?" For some reason, her grandfather's reply was terribly important to Summer.

"Why, they sat down with me," he answered. "What difference does it make?"

"I just wondered," Summer answered. "I didn't want David to feel funny . . . since we aren't dating anymore."

"That Ann girl have an eye ailment?"

Summer turned to her grandfather with a frown. When he saw he had her complete attention, he started batting his eyelashes in a furious effort and Summer broke into gales of laughter. His imitation of Ann was priceless.

"The boys all seem to like the way Ann flirts," Summer said. "I think she looks like she has a problem."

"Your claws are showing, kitten," her grandfather admonished. "You're very pretty, as pretty as Ann, and you're Irish besides. David will come around. You mark my words."

Wishful thinking, Summer concluded.

"Just hope you find a little confidence in yourself soon, girl. After you win the race, we'll have to concentrate on that area."

"So I'm going to win the race, am I?" Summer teased.

"Of course," her grandfather answered immediately. "Bet a fiver on you with Clancy.

Easy money. Course I had to talk him into betting against you. He finally gave in though."

"I think I have a good chance," Summer said, "but I haven't seen the competition. They might all be pros."

"Nope. The pros, as you call them, don't stand a chance against you. Now, I've got a few suggestions for increasing your speed just a wee bit more. . . ."

"Summer! Wait up a minute!" The summons came from David.

Summer and Grandfather both turned and watched David jog towards them. Summer couldn't keep the surprise out of her expression and saw that her grandfather wore a very smug expression he didn't try to hide.

"Hi, David," Summer said in a breathless little voice.

David didn't smile. He seemed to be having a little trouble looking directly at her, too. He seemed downright fascinated with the top of her head, staring intently at her bangs. Summer reacted by trying to puff her hair up a little with her hand.

"Listen, you did say you were going to help with the project, and I've got over thirty posters that need to be delivered. Ann's going to take ten and I'll do ten and — "

"I'll be happy to take ten," Summer interjected. "Anything else?"

"Well, the T-shirts are just sitting in boxes at Ann's house. She was supposed to sell them yesterday at the grocery store but she couldn't. Ann's very busy, you know," he added.

Sure, she is, Summer thought. She's always busy when real work is involved. "Look, David, maybe Regina and I could sell them this Saturday." A sudden inspiration penetrated Summer's brain. "Uh, you know, that is, Regina is going to have this party and if I bring the T-shirts, maybe I could talk some of the kids into buying them. Regina could even make it a T-shirt party or something."

David perked up over that suggestion. "When is it?"

"Next Friday — no, I mean it's next Saturday, I think. I'll have to check with Regina and let you know."

"I should probably go to Regina's party," David said. "Since I'm in charge of the T-shirts, that would probably be the smart thing to do." He was addressing her feet now, having apparently lost interest in her hair and still unable to look her right in the eye.

"Oh, I agree," Summer said a little more enthusiastically than she intended.

"I'll come by tomorrow with your ten posters and you can let me know when the party is."

"Fine."

"You might as well ride with me to deliver the posters."

Summer nodded and David left. Grandpa started in chuckling and Summer frowned over his reaction. He never said a word about the conversation, only gave her a broad wink that told her he was mighty pleased.

The rest of the trip home was spent discussing Summer's strategy for increasing her running speed. Summer barely listened, planning her own strategy with one David Marshall.

When the pair entered the house, Summer's mother was so relieved that Grandfather was behaving rationally, that she hugged him and planted a big kiss on his ruddy cheek.

"Read my notes before you get yourself all worked up," her grandfather chided. His expression was firm, but the gentleness in his voice suggested he liked the fact that she was concerned for him.

Summer felt very close to her family all of a sudden. They were caring people, and even if they were a little nutty most of the time, they belonged to her and no one, not even Ann Logan, could take them away.

"Summer, please help me set the table," her mother asked.

"She needs to call Regina first," Grandfather interjected with a wide grin.

"Why?" Summer and her mother asked in unison.

"Don't you need to tell her she's having a party?"

# $E$leven

David rang the doorbell of Summer's house. He was loaded down with posters.

"Do you have time to go with me now and deliver some of the posters?" he asked.

"Of course," Summer said, but she tried to keep her expression neutral.

They made two stops, the first at the bank and the second at a dry cleaners, before David said a single word. "What's that book you've got with you?"

"It's a joke book," Summer explained. "There are some really great jokes in here," she lied. Well, she told herself, it wasn't an actual lie. She hadn't had time to open the book but she was sure it had wonderful jokes inside. "Want me to read some of them to you?" she suggested in an eager voice.

David agreed and Summer immediately began reading. She could tell, after the third joke, that David was beginning to relax and enjoy himself. She considered switching the subject to their fight and was trying to figure out how she could apologize for yelling at him — and lying to him — without groveling when David launched into a rather long joke of his own.

Summer decided that no matter what, she was going to love his joke. As soon as David paused, Summer laughed. She even dabbed at her eyes the way she had noticed Ann did when she laughed and thought that she was doing a good job of faking it.

"You're supposed to wait for the punch line before you laugh," David told her. He was looking at her like she had one too many heads, and Summer wanted to slip under the seat.

They didn't say another word until all the posters had been delivered and they were back in front of Summer's house.

"The party is Saturday night," Summer mumbled as she opened the car door. "Don't forget to bring the T-shirts."

"Okay," David said.

He smiled and Summer decided to go for broke. "David, if you want, you could go to the party with me. I'll help you carry in the boxes of T-shirts and . . . stuff."

David looked embarrassed and Summer wanted to kick herself. "Ann already suggested that we go together. I told her about the party," he explained in a halting voice.

"Right." Summer couldn't get out another word. She nodded good-bye and started running towards the house.

"Summer? We could come by and pick you up," David yelled.

"That's okay," Summer said. "Uh . . . Gregg asked me to be his date but I thought I would help you out with the T-shirts and all. I'll just call him back and tell him okay. No big deal, David. See you."

She wasn't even able to wait until she got to the bedroom. She was crying before she reached the front door.

"Summer, you've got to come over here and see me. I look great!" The boast was bellowed through the phone the next afternoon.

"Then a miracle has happened. Did you just get back from Lourdes?"

"Very funny," Regina replied. "I got my hair cut and it looks wonderful."

"Terrific," Summer muttered. "Look, Regina, I'm in a terrible mood. The whole family is hiding from me. If I come over I'll ruin our friendship."

"Don't argue. Come over and tell me what's happening."

Summer did exactly that and had to admit that, after pouring out her heart to Regina, she did feel a little better.

"Do you or do you not want David back?" Regina demanded.

"I do," Summer admitted. "But I don't know why. He's stubborn and — "

"Enough of that," Regina stated. "We'll plan our strategy. He's coming to the party, right?"

"With Ann," Summer reminded her friend.

"Okay," Regina replied. "I seem to remember your telling me that you were going to become a flirt and dethrone Ann. The party's a good time. I'm going to ask Luke to be my date," she added.

"You'll look smashing with your new hair cut," Summer said. Regina did look good. Gone were the long, limp curls, replaced by short, feathered layers that ended just below Regina's delicate ears. Whenever Regina moved, which was all the time, her hair swooshed back and forth and then settled back into position.

Regina's enthusiasm was contagious. "Confidence is the name of the game," Summer stated. "That's what Ann has and I'm going to get."

"How?"

"That's the tricky part, Regina," Summer admitted. "I'm not sure. . . ."

"I always feel more confident if I'm wearing something new. Let's buy new outfits for the party."

"Okay," Summer agreed. "We'll go shopping tomorrow."

"Remember, Saturday is D-Day," Regina announced. She sounded just like a general.

# Twelve

"Mom, could I get a loan?" Summer waited while her mother dried her hands on the dish towel before rushing into her prepared explanation. It wouldn't be half as convincing unless she had her mother's full attention.

"Regina is having a party and I don't have a thing to wear," she began. "I'll pay you back real soon."

"You don't have to pay me back, Summer. You've been such a help. This will be my treat."

"Honest?" It was manna from heaven, this unexpected development, but Summer wanted to make sure. "I thought we were poor," she said.

"We aren't poor, honey," her mother answered. "Just frugal. Your father works hard for his income and I want to stretch it. I'll give you some money tomorrow."

Regina's mother insisted on driving Regina and Summer to the mall.

"I'll pick you both up in exactly two hours. If you can't find something suitable to wear in that amount of time, it's just too bad," she told the girls.

"Mom, quit treating me like a baby. I'm fifteen," Regina said.

"Now behave yourselves."

"Yes, Mrs. Muntz," Summer answered. She used the same tone of voice she used when talking to her own mother, for Summer had realized a long time ago that all mothers were basically alike. They all loved to worry and give orders, and they all said the same things.

"Your mother is a carbon copy of mine," Summer said when she and Regina walked into the mall. "Do you suppose they all read a special manual or something before they have children, so they all say the same things?"

Regina laughed and nodded. "All mothers have the same traits, and they're all hung up on hygiene. Ever notice that?"

"You mean, 'brush your teeth,' 'comb your hair'?"

"Exactly," Regina replied. "And they all go crazy if they find any holes in anything — especially underwear."

"Regina, that's disgusting. True, but disgusting."

"Heaven forbid if I was in an accident and had on anything with holes in it. Whatever would the doctors say?"

"Tears, rips, holes," Summer said, "are a

125

direct reflection of incompetent motherhood."

Borgen's, an elegant department store, was the first store they planned to hit, and both girls grew silent as they hurried toward their target. Regina found just the outfit, a lovely lavender jump suit that zipped up the front.

"You look good," Summer said, and meant every word. Regina did look spectacular.

It took another hour of hunting and digging before Summer found her dream. It was a pale pink sun dress that flattered her tan. Summer felt quite sophisticated as she stood in front of the dressing room mirror, one hand holding the thick mass of hair atop her head.

"What do you think?" she asked her friend. "Will I do?"

"We are going to knock 'em dead."


As soon as Summer returned home, she changed into her new dress and modeled "the new Summer" in front of an admiring grandfather and her parents. "I've completed my transformation," Summer informed her family at the dinner table. "The old Summer is gone."

"What's all this about change?" her grandfather asked.

"I've decided you were right, Grandfather. I did lack confidence, so I decided to change myself."

"You still haven't gotten the point," her grandfather said with a shake of his head.

"We'll talk about it on the way to bingo. Better get moving."

Grandfather showed his disappointment during the walk to the church. "You've completely sidestepped the issue. Or perhaps you just don't understand what I've been trying to say to you, child. I want you to be happy with you, not flit around trying to change this and that. You are special just as you are, and until you believe that, no matter what changes you make, you'll always feel unhappy. Celebrate who *you* are. Realize there is only one Summer Matthews. Only then can you share your specialness with anyone else."

Summer mulled over her grandfather's words. "It's hard," she whispered.

"You mean it's much easier to envy someone else?"

"I guess so."

"The grass isn't always greener on the other side of the fence."

"Meaning?"

"Well, this Ann person. Are you so sure you want to be like her?"

"Sort of," Summer hedged.

"Have you ever considered that maybe she isn't all that happy? Never hope to change places with someone else. They have just as many problems — maybe different problems, but problems all the same."

Summer hadn't thought of that angle.

"How many times have I said that you should count your blessings?"

"Lots," Summer answered.

While she continued to listen to her grandfather's quiet encouragement, a part of her was preoccupied with the thought that David might be helping Mr. Clancy again. Her fingers crossed in hopefulness when she and grandfather walked into the church hall.

He wasn't there, and her disappointment was almost overwhelming. By the time intermission began, Summer had accepted the fact that David wasn't going to show up. For that reason, when she turned to refill the coffee pot, she almost jumped when she saw David leaning against the door frame watching her. She couldn't stop the smile of greeting but it quickly faded when she saw the hesitancy in his eyes.

"Hello, Summer. Sorry I'm late."

"Don't worry. Lots of people don't come until the second half. That's when the big bingo games are played. Your grandfather? . . ."

"He didn't come tonight." David seemed embarrassed with that admission. "But I thought I'd drop by and see if you needed any help."

"You really want to help?" Summer was singing inside. She knew she sounded incredulous, but couldn't seem to help it.

"Sure," David answered. "I'll do that for you," he added, taking the coffeepot from Summer. "Where's Mr. Clancy?"

"He went to get some more paper cups. It's a full house tonight. There's a five-thousand dollar cash prize on the last bingo if anyone wins before seventy numbers have been called. Of course, the odds are impossible but the lure brings everybody out."

"Ann suggested that you and Gregg might want to double with us Saturday night. What do you say?"

Summer didn't know how to reply, what to say, and luckily Mr. Clancy appeared just at that moment. "David, good to see you," he said in an enthusiastic voice. "And just in time. Help me serve this coffee before the big jackpot starts."

The next twenty minutes were busy. David stopped Summer in the middle of scrubbing the popcorn vat with a tap on her shoulder. "What about doubling?"

"No," Summer answered. "I promised to help Regina, so Gregg is picking me up early," she lied. Was he really that dense? Summer asked herself. Didn't he know how miserable she would be watching him with Ann? Why, she would rather stay home than be subjected to that scene! All hopes that David cared for her at all vanished. He was obviously under Ann's spell. It was hopeless.

"Will you save a dance for me Saturday?" he asked.

"Of course," Summer answered. "I'm sure Gregg won't mind." Now why had she added that? she asked herself. She saw the hesitancy creep into David's eyes and was surprised by it.

"Fine," was all that he said, but that one word was terribly flat.

The big jackpot started, and silence, except for the numbers being called, reigned. It was the last game, and as soon as the seventy numbers were called, she would find her grandfather and head home.

Summer waited with her arms folded, leaning against the window pane, for Mrs. Willkin's ritualistic, See you next week, ladies and gentlemen. Instead, she heard her grandfather's jubilant bellow, "Bingo!"

It took a full minute for Summer to register the fact that her grandfather had just won a huge amount of money, and then she was jumping up and down and clapping at the same time. Everyone was thrilled. David hugged her and so did Mr. Clancy.

"That Irish rascal deserves to win," Mr. Clancy announced.

When Summer finally reached her beaming grandfather, she hugged him and giggled with delight. "What are you going to do with all that money, Grandpa?" she asked when Mrs. Willkins handed him the cashier's check.

"I've grand plans, my girl, grand plans. I'm giving some of the money to your father, just for the sheer pleasure of the deed," he explained on the way home. "And I'm going to take a trip to Ireland with the rest."

"Ireland?"

"It's not a fact, yet. Your mother and father might give me a hard time but I long for Dublin's green, Summer. Ah, child, the grass of Ireland is like no other. The leprechaun's surely had a hand in farming the land."

"I hope Mom and Dad are still awake. They'll be so excited for you, but I bet Daddy won't take any of the money. Mother says we aren't really poor, just frugal."

All the lights were on in the house when Grandfather and Summer hurried toward the door. Michael's sobs could be heard from the porch. "Mick must be coming down with something," her grandfather said with a frown.

Summer's father was busy rocking a distressed Michael in the squeaky rocking chair but stopped the motion when she and Grandfather entered the living room.

"Have a good time, Dad?" her father asked Grandpa.

"You could say that, my boy," her grandfather replied with a twinkle in his eyes. "Now give me my grandson and I'll tell you what happened tonight."

Michael immediately slipped off his father's lap and stretched his arms out to his grandfather. It was a fact that he liked to cuddle up against his grandfather, and loved to listen to the stories his grandfather had a special way of telling.

Michael's face was all flushed. "You look terrible," Summer said to her little brother, and only then realized it wasn't the right thing to say to a three-year-old.

Michael promptly started wailing again.

"He's got a bit of a fever, that's all," her mother said from the doorway. "Probably just the flu," she added.

Grandfather patted Michael and began to rock him. "I've won the jackpot, children."

The reaction was instantaneous. Everyone began to talk at once. When the cheers had quieted, and her grandfather had outlined his intent to give Summer's parents part of the money, her father declined.

"But if I'm ever strapped for money, I won't hesitate to ask you for a loan," her father said.

"All right, I won't pressure you," Grandfather answered. "But it's there when you need it. By the way," he added, winking at Summer, "I'm going to take a little trip with some of the money."

"Oh?" Both Summer's father and mother seemed surprised with that information, and Summer noticed the funny look that passed between the two of them. Summer didn't understand why they would be anything but delighted. After all, it was Grandfather's winnings, and he was an adult. He certainly didn't need their permission to take a trip.

"To Ireland," her grandfather said.

"But Dad!"

"Yes, son?" Grandfather's voice sounded very calm.

"Ireland is so far away," he replied, "and I don't like the idea of you traveling halfway around the world all by yourself. If anything happened, you'd be all alone."

Now Summer began to understand. Both her mother and her father were concerned that Grandfather would go into one of his confused spells. She hadn't considered that aspect!

"Mr. Clancy!" Summer blurted the name into the tension-filled room and then giggled at the look of surprise and delight her grandfather sent her way.

"Now why didn't I think of that?" he asked with a chuckle. "John hails from Ireland and I know he longs to return, just as I do. But I was thinking of taking you, Summer. After all, you are family."

Summer knew that Grandfather would prefer Mr. Clancy's companionship and didn't hesitate to say so. "I can see Ireland later, Grandpa. Mr. Clancy is such a good friend of yours. I mean, I'd like to go, but he doesn't have much time left."

Oh, Summer thought, I've said it all wrong. She looked at her mother for some support before adding, "And I couldn't go into all those pubs you keep telling me about. You'd worry that I was bored, and I'd worry that you weren't doing what you wanted to do."

"You're a very special child," her grandfather said. His voice was full of praise and love, and Summer felt like she had a halo over her head. Honesty nudged her from her vision of sainthood. She really didn't want to go to Ireland all that much. Too many important things were happening now, and she didn't want to miss any of them.

"Does that stop your worrying?" her grandfather asked Summer's father.

"Now, Dad, I wasn't really worried, just concerned. If John Clancy will go with you, I admit, I'd feel a whole lot better."

"Then it's settled. Now let's get this little imp off to bed."

"Grandpa," Summer asked in a whisper, "you won't leave for Ireland before my race will you?"

"*Our* race, Summer," her grandfather corrected. "And I wouldn't even consider leaving before then."

"Good," Summer sighed. It was very important that her grandpa be there — very important, indeed.

"Just nine more days, sweetheart, and victory will be yours."

"You're so sure I'm going to win?" Summer teased.

"Just by running, you're victorious. That's what we will celebrate. Should you win . . . well then, that will just be the frosting on the cake."

"I don't understand," Summer said.

"No, I know you don't, but someday you will, Summer."

Summer thought over her grandfather's words for over an hour, but couldn't reconcile his feelings about the unimportance of winning. Wasn't the saying, Winning isn't everything, it's the only thing, true?

The sounds of crying from her parent's room interrupted Summer's introspection. Michael was keeping her parents awake, for at his insistence, he had been allowed to sleep with them. His insistence had actually been a full-blown tantrum.

Summer dragged herself out of bed and went to her parents' room. "Mike, come on and sleep with me," she said, taking pity on her exhausted-looking parents. "I'll rub your back."

Five minutes later, Michael was snuggled against Summer and the heat from his fever felt like Summer was wrapped in a heating blanket. Summer rubbed his back until he fell into a fitful sleep.

When she opened her eyes the next morning, Michael was just inches from her face, staring intently into her eyes.

"I'm all well," he announced with a grin, but Summer, once she was able to focus, had to disagree.

"Michael, you're covered with spots! Go and look in the mirror!" The surprise in her voice triggered alarm in Michael's eyes. Summer quickly recovered and forced a smile. "Are you ever lucky! Now you'll get lots of presents and treats when Mom sees you."

If Michael was anything, he was definitely mercenary. The grin returned and he bounded off the bed, running to find his mother. The sooner she saw the spots, the better.

"Chicken pox," her mother announced at the breakfast table.

"He looks funny," Summer said when Michael left the room.

"Summer, honey," her mother began, "there's no easy way to tell you this. But you've never had the chicken pox, either."

"What?" The one word was a scream of distress but her mother reacted sympathetically, reaching across the table and patting Summer's hand.

"But the race!"

"Now let's see, the race is eight days away, and there's a seven- to ten-day span before you break out . . . provided you were just exposed, that is. . . ."

"Mother, this is horrible."

"Now, Summer, let's not borrow trouble. How do you feel?"

"Fine." Summer answered.

"Maybe you're not going to get them. Oh dear, I don't know."

"Mother, if there's a seven-day waiting period, I could break out right before the race." Even as she said the words, the full realization that all her hard work could go right down the drain hit her like a slap in the face.

"It's useless to worry, Summer. There isn't anything we can do about it. Just say a prayer and cross your fingers. It will all work out."

"Fat chance with my luck," Summer muttered. "Just watch, I'll get sick the morning of the race. I can't run with a fever and spots," she moaned.

"Not everyone gets as sick as Michael. You might just have a little rash, and no fever at all. Of course, you still couldn't run."

Ironic, Summer decided. When she had first started to run, she would have welcomed the chicken pox, or even a plague for that matter — anything for an excuse not to compete. Well, that situation had changed! Now, Summer would do anything in order to run.

Regina was borderline sympathetic when Summer told her the news about Michael. "Just be happy you don't have them now. You'd miss my party," she explained.

Summer didn't tell Regina that she would rather miss the party than the race, for she knew Regina would never understand.

# *T*hirteen

It wasn't until the morning of the big day, Regina's party, that Summer remembered what she had told David. Grandfather's windfall must have pushed that thought aside. Now she realized that she had told him that Gregg would be her date tonight.

Panic that she couldn't talk Gregg into it, or that he already had a date, made dialing the phone a bit awkward. After two attempts, she finally had Regina on the line.

"I told David I had a date with Gregg. How are we going to talk Gregg into it?

"That was good thinking," Regina replied, "to make David think you and Gregg are an item. I think he has a date to go to the movies with Marilyn McGuire, but I'm not sure."

"Oh, heavens, what are we going to do?"

"Summer, don't get all upset. We're dealing with Gregg, remember?"

"And?" Summer answered, hope entering her tone.

"We can get him to do anything we want. Trust me."

"How?" Summer demanded.

"Money, of course. Gregg is always broke."

"But if he has a date — "

"Summer," Regina groaned in exasperation, "we're talking about Gregg. He'll give up a date with Miss America if the price is right."

A half hour later Gregg called, sounding very miffed.

"Thirty dollars! Gregg, that's too much," Summer yelped.

"Take it or leave it," Gregg returned. "My car needs a new muffler and I have to placate Marilyn. Heck, she's going to be as mad as a hornet. You're getting a real deal."

"Well, I can't pay you more than ten dollars tonight, but I'll have the rest soon. I promise."

Summer's mind was racing with ideas of where she would ever dredge up another twenty dollars, and she was bordering on acute despair until she heard her grandfather's voice in the background.

Her grandfather was in a generous mood. Instead of giving her the ten dollars she asked for, he gave her the full amount when she explained the reason for the emergency loan. Still, his obvious displeasure with the entire situation was unmistakable.

"You are actually going to pay a boy to take you to a party?"

"It's not a boy, it's Gregg," Summer reasoned. "And it isn't like it sounds."

"Times have certainly changed since I was a lad. Why, I can't imagine your grandmother, bless her soul, ever paying for an escort."

"Well, this is a unique situation. I just got trapped in a . . . story, and I'm trying to save face."

"But who trapped you? Answer me that?"

"Grandpa, you sound like I'm doing something illegal. It's no big deal. You just don't understand. And I'm the one who got myself trapped into this."

"Exactly. You might not be doing anything against the law, but it certainly isn't very truthful, is it?"

"No." Summer gave up trying to make him understand. He did have a valid point, though.

Summer soaked a long while in the scented bubble bath before she dressed for Regina's party. She forced the cobwebs of excuses from her mind. Her grandfather was right. Since meeting David, Summer had done nothing but lie. And that first little half truth, that lie, like a tiny snowball beginning its trek down the steep mountain, had gathered force and grown awesome in size, until it threatened terrible damage. Summer had become trapped in one deception after another, and each little white lie had grown just as immense as the innocent snowball. It was time for her to stop. The lies were becoming too easy, and the fear that she would some-day be unable to tell the difference, to dis-tinguish truth from deceit, frightened her. Besides, trying to remember what story she had told required stamina. Most of all, even though she had been able to squeeze through one situation after another, she didn't feel very happy about it — or herself.

If the arrangement hadn't already been made with Gregg, Summer decided she would have just gone to Regina's party alone. So what if Ann gloated. Ann was Ann, and the sooner Summer recognized that fact, the better. But Gregg had already broken his date with Marilyn to go with her, so Summer would have to go through this one last de-ception. Tonight would be the last time she would trap herself. *No more lies!*

When she finished with her bath, Summer felt just as clean on the inside as she did on the outside now that she had resolved to be herself. All those silly deceptions. . . . Sum-mer decided they were just walls she had built so that people couldn't get a glimpse of the real her. If she acted like someone else, or told stories about herself that weren't true, then the rejections could always be excused. "Guess I am growing wise in my old age," Summer told Michael. He was sit-ting on her bed, scratching, while Summer set her hair in hot curlers.

"You look pretty," Michael praised her when Summer was finished.

"Thank you, Michael," Summer replied. She twirled in front of the mirror and smiled. "I do at that," she added to herself.

# *Fourteen*

Summer was combing her hair again when her grandfather's voice called. "Summer? Your escort is here."

Gregg looked a little embarrassed. He wasn't even cleaned up. Just wearing a pair of clean jeans and an Ohio University sweat shirt, but his hair was combed. That ought to count for something, Summer concluded.

"I hate to ask," Gregg said immediately, "but do you have the ten dollars?"

"Better," Summer replied. "I've got the entire amount."

"That's great," Gregg said. "And that entitles you to the full treatment."

"What does that mean?"

"I won't leave your side. I promise. Look Summer, I kind of . . . well, I'm a little embarrassed to take your money."

"Well, in that case. . . ." Summer reached

to take back the money, but Gregg quickly snatched his hand away.

"Not that embarrassed," he qualified. "But don't worry. You'll get your money's worth, kid."

The one bright spot in an otherwise horrible evening was Regina. It was, without a doubt, her finest hour! She looked just like a vision. The boys were divided into two camps. Ann had her following, and *Regina* was surrounded by the others. Best of all, several of the faithful-to-Ann boys deserted her in favor of Regina's ready smile.

Summer was proud of herself. She wasn't jealous at all. Her friendship overruled such a reaction. Regina deserved to be the belle of the ball, as her grandfather would say. And she really did look lovely. The most amazing thing was that her tall friend was standing straight. Her slouching seemed to be a thing of the past.

Summer stayed as far away from David and Ann as she could. It would be difficult keeping the pain of David's abandonment from showing in her eyes. At one point, Ann was on her way toward Summer when Regina "accidentally" nudged Carl Benson into the pool. The timing was superb and Ann forgot all about Summer.

Regina had her little streak of revenge. Summer had no doubt that the little push was her way of getting even for Carl's past deception.

"Shame on you, Regina," Summer said

with a sparkle in her eyes. "That wasn't very nice."

"But it was an accident," Regina replied. "A splendid accident." Both girls giggled hysterically.

"Remember who you're talking to, Regina. And I have a new rule, one you should adopt. No more lies. No matter how insignificant."

"You're kidding!" Regina seemed astonished.

"No, I mean it. From now on I tell the truth."

"Won't that be boring?"

"Boring? Telling the truth will be refreshing. Lies get too confusing."

"Bet you can't do it," Regina challenged.

"Bet *you* can't," Summer responded.

"Oh yeah? I can do anything you can do."

"Starting when?"

"Right now. By the way," Regina said, "David was looking for you a few minutes ago. He doesn't seem all that interested in Ann."

"I don't know how you can say that. She's always hanging on him."

"Exactly my point. Have you ever seen David hanging on her?"

"You're just being technical, Regina. He must like it or he wouldn't keep going out with her."

"Maybe she's always asking him. Ever think of that angle?"

"Fat chance. You're just grasping at straws," Summer said pessimistically.

145

"Here comes Luke. Doesn't he look fantastic?" Regina sighed.

"Yes, he does," Summer replied. "I'll fade into the crowd so you can be alone with him for a few minutes."

"David really did ask me about you," Regina called softly. "Go and see what he wants."

Telling David that Regina said he wanted to see her was a good excuse to talk to him, Summer decided. She thought she saw Ann go into the house, alone, so she hurried to find David.

When she found him, she would talk to him about the race, and then her grandfather's latest project, and what he was going to do with his bingo money. She felt very confident.

When she spotted David, the confidence, like a balloon, burst.

He wasn't alone. Ann was with him, her arms wrapped around his neck — and they were kissing!

Summer turned and started back toward the crowd. But she couldn't help taking one more peek, and her gaze clashed with David's. Did time stop while they stared at each other? Summer knew it hadn't, and that they had just looked at each other for the barest of seconds, yet it seemed an eternity. Did he see the hurt in her eyes? Summer hoped not.

Marching back toward the group, Summer muttered to herself, "A lost cause." Waterlogged Carl Benson heard her.

"You lost something?" he asked.

"No." For a fleeting second Summer considered pushing Carl back into the pool, but quickly squelched that uncharitable thought. "Want to dance?" she asked, feeling sorry for the dripping mass in front of her.

"Sure, if you don't mind getting a little wet," Carl replied.

They danced to a slow song, one of Summer's favorites, but the melody was ruined by the persistent squish of Carl's soggy tennis shoes.

"May I cut in?" The formal request came from behind and both Carl and Summer turned.

David didn't wait for an answer from Carl. He just took hold of Summer's hand and pulled her into his arms.

The music took on a whole new feeling. Summer tried to remain stiff and formal in David's arms but she wanted to just melt against him and put her head on his shoulder. The picture of David and Ann kissing kept her from making a fool of herself.

"Where's Ann? Repairing her lipstick?" Summer asked.

"It was just a little kiss. . . ."

"Could have fooled me. I thought she had fainted and you were giving her mouth-to-mouth resuscitation."

"It wasn't like that," David said. "Summer, she was kissing me and I was just being . . . passive."

"If that was passive, you must be a crazed

maniac when you actively kiss someone."

"Well, I kissed you. Was I a maniac?"

"No," Summer muttered. "But you shouldn't bring that up. It's old business."

"No it isn't, unless you're really serious about Gregg."

The music ended before Summer could answer David.

Carl joined them and asked, "Are you guys all set for next Saturday?"

"Next Saturday?" Summer asked, puzzled.

"The race, Summer," David explained.

"Oh yes, the race," Summer mumbled. "I don't know if I'm all set or not."

"You're set," Luke said, coming to stand beside her. "David, have you ever run with Summer?"

"No."

"Well, she's really something. I think she has a real chance to win."

"I don't know. David, I've never run in a race before and I don't know what to expect. I'm a little nervous," Summer said with complete, utterly refreshing honesty.

"Why are you so nervous about the race?" David whispered when Luke was talking to Carl.

"I just don't know how fast everyone else is going to be. I might be left at the gate. That would be embarrassing."

"Run with me! I think I'm a pretty good judge, and I've been in several races."

"I'd like that," Summer replied.

"How about tomorrow?" David asked. "I

could pick you up or meet you at the park."
His voice sounded shy. Was he unsure of her
answer? Impossible, Summer told herself.

"Why don't you pick me up around eight.
Okay?"

"Great," David said.

Summer hoped that the "great" was because he wanted to be with her, but that idea
was stopped with his next sentence.

"How about asking your grandfather to
come along. I've got a stopwatch and if he
wouldn't mind, he could pace us."

"Pace us?"

"You know, sit on a bench at the starting
point and time us, help us with our pace."

"I still don't understand," Summer said.
"How can he help us with our pace?"

"By figuring out when we need to push,
when to put the spurt on," David explained
patiently.

"I don't think I have a spurt," Summer
said. "I just run."

"You keep the same pace the entire time?"
David was genuinely surprised with her information.

"Summer, everyone knows how to pace
themselves, when to put the push on."

"I don't," Summer said, grinning. "David,
I've made a pact with myself. I'm never telling another lie, no matter what."

"Why did you lie to me about running?" he
asked.

Summer took a deep breath and then
plunged in. "I was jealous of Ann. She was

hanging all over you and I wanted to impress you."

David seemed shocked but also happy with her admission. He opened his mouth to say something and then closed it. This telling the truth business wasn't all that bad. "The funny thing is that I hated running at first, and now I can't seem to get through a day unless I put in eight miles," she told him.

"It gets in your blood." David understood, but then he was a runner, too.

"There you are, David." Ann came and stood next to David and Summer sighed.

"Did you need something, Ann?" David asked.

"You promised me this dance," Ann said with a forced pout. She must practice before a mirror, Summer thought. Ann glared at Summer and Summer wondered if Ann could read her mind. Still, there was a tinge of victory in that glare as far as Summer was concerned. Mount Olympus just might be trembling, and if it was, Ann would soon be toppled from her position. Regina had started the tremors in her competitive bid to match Ann, and Summer was going to do the same.

"A promise is a promise," Summer said to David. "Thank you for the dance," she added before slowly walking away.

Gregg found Summer, gloating, and told her they were supposed to dance. "Orders from the boss."

"Regina?" Summer asked.

"Who else. She told me I should kiss you

when David's looking, but that will cost you an extra ten."

"Thanks anyway," Summer said. "Don't drool over me anymore. Just one dance and you can split."

"How will you get home?" Summer thought that the expression on Gregg's face resembled a man who had just received a stay of execution.

"Maybe Luke or Carl will give me a ride."

"No, I better drive you home. Otherwise you might want some of your money back."

"Always the gentleman," Summer replied. "I don't want to dance. Come on," she said, linking her arm through his in a sisterly fashion, "let's go inside. I'll watch you eat for a while."

Summer witnessed Gregg devour three huge slices of pizza before the party ended. She helped Regina clean up while she listened to her friend tell her all about Luke. When Regina finally wound down, Summer told her about her talk with David.

"So you have a date tomorrow, then?" Regina asked.

"Not a date, Regina," Summer corrected. "And Grandfather is coming along. Besides, Ann told Carl that she and David were going steady."

"Ha!" Regina snorted. "That's all in her mind. She's feeling threatened . . . just like we've felt in the past with her."

"I don't think she was making it up. I saw David kissing her earlier. Regina, I just have to accept the fact that David doesn't care for me other than as a friend. That's why he's going to run with me tomorrow. He's just a nice person."

"I think you're wrong. Oh, David is nice enough. But I think he really cares about you."

"You're just saying that because you have to. It goes with being my friend."

"Well, if you feel it's all a lost cause, then why are you running in the race?"

"Two reasons," Summer explained. "One, because I want to win. I love running, Regina. I know you can't understand that, but I *do* love the challenge."

"And the second reason?"

"Because of Ann. She still thinks I'll back out before the race. Guess I want to show her."

"Did Luke tell you what she said?"

"No, what?"

"He said that Ann told Carl and some other kids that you haven't done any running at all and that she just knew you would find an excuse on the day of the race not to show up."

"Did Luke tell her he's seen me running almost every day?"

"No, he was too surprised by what she was saying. And then, he said he decided to let her find out for herself how good you are. Those were his exact words." Regina glowed, her infatuation with Luke obvious.

"Well, nothing will keep me from showing up."

"That's the spirit."

"Except . . ."

"Don't say it. Don't even think it. . . ."

"What?" Gregg asked from the doorway.

"Chicken pox," both girls replied at the same time.

# Fifteen

Excitement, rather than the alarm clock, woke Summer the next morning. Soon she would be seeing David, and even if it was only friendship on his part, Summer was thrilled just the same.

Michael threw another tantrum when he was informed that he couldn't go to the park, but his mother held fast.

Summer wore a pair of white shorts and a new navy-blue tank top. She didn't have a matching headband, so she settled on a bright red one. "I look like the flag," she told her mother.

David looked great, too. He had on a pair of gold jogging shorts and a black top. The colors looked good against his tanned skin, and if Summer had been a bold person, she would have complimented David on his good-looking legs.

Grandfather fiddled with the stopwatch

David insisted he use, until he felt confident with the dials.

Summer climbed into the backseat of David's car so Grandfather could sit in the front and listened while David explained pacing to him.

When Grandpa was settled on the bench next to the entrance of the park, and David and Summer were ready to start, Summer turned to David and squared her shoulders.

"David, I'm not into lies anymore," she said, "so get this good and clear. I'm going to do my darnedest to beat you. I'm not going to hold back because I'm a girl and you're a boy. If you have a problem with that, tell me now." Her hands were settled on her hips during her lecture and she waited impatiently for his answer.

David started laughing. "And I was going to tell you how I've been running a lot longer than you have and not to be too upset when I beat you. Think you're that good, huh?"

"Yep," Summer answered.

"Yeah?"

"Yeah! Winner throws the loser in the pool?"

"You got it," David said, grinning. "And the loser can take her tennis shoes off before she gets all wet, okay?"

"We'll see, David," Summer said, turning back to Grandpa. "Guess we're ready when you are, Grandpa."

When Grandfather yelled go, both David and Summer took off in a flash of speed. Summer stayed right beside him until they had gone four miles. David's pace began to slacken then, and Summer flashed him a smile as she sailed in front of him. She could hear him behind her until that last mile began, and then suddenly Summer saw him gain on her out of the corner of her eye. She increased her speed accordingly, matching him stride for stride, until Grandfather's form came into sight. Then David really put a spurt on, and Summer knew in that instant what pacing was all about. She pulled from her hidden reserve all the extra energy she could muster, winnning by several lengths.

"Did you hold back or did I win fair and square?" she asked David when she could get her breath.

"No, you really did keep me pushing," David answered. "I tried to save a little something for that last mile, but I guess you saved a little more."

"Race you to the pool?" David said.

"You're on," Summer answered, charging ahead of him. She ran as fast as she could until she came to the edge of the pool.

David came to stand beside her, panting for breath. His hands were on his hips, and his body was covered with a film of perspiration, giving Summer the evidence that he had run as fast and as hard as he could.

She watched as he untied his shoes laces and kicked off his shoes. If a boy could swagger, David did, as he walked to the deep end of the pool and positioned himself on the ledge, facing her. His arms were folded across his chest and he had a silly expression on his face.

Summer slipped off her own shoes, intent on just getting her feet wet in the shallow end of the pool. Then she too swaggered up to stand directly in front of David.

"Ah, poor David," she teased. "The agony of defeat," she said, placing her index finger on his chest. She was savoring her victory and gloating all at the same time. Still, she did notice a wicked gleam in David's eyes, but before she could figure out just what he was thinking, he grabbed hold of her shoulders and pulled her towards him.

Summer squealed when David lost his balance, and she just had time to close her mouth and take a deep breath before they both hit the water.

Summer came up sputtering. Talk about sore losers! She would certainly tell him a thing or two — when he quit laughing, that is.

"You're crazy, David," Summer said while she treaded water. She swung out and tried to make it to the safe side of the pool but David grabbed her from behind and dunked her, and that was the start of war. Summer splashed in retaliation, trying to dunk him, but he was too fast.

Exhaustion made Summer give up the game after a few minutes.

"David, let me get out. I'm going to drown."

"Don't worry. I'll revive you. I know how. I teach swimming, remember?"

She remembered all right. She remembered how he had kissed Ann. "Like you revived Ann the other night?" Summer muttered softly enough that she was sure David hadn't heard.

"Why are you frowning?" David asked as he pulled her out of the pool.

"I was just thinking that we're going to ruin your car with our wet clothes. Maybe we should drip dry first."

"Don't have time," David answered. "I have an appointment with — "

"Never mind," Summer interrupted, instinctively knowing who the appointment was with. "Let's get my grandpa so you won't be late for your date."

David didn't deny that he had a date, and that made Summer sure she was right! She tried to act very blasé, keeping her face shielded from David while she wrung out the bottom of her tank top. Modesty prevented her from doing more.

They walked in silence to the car, both barefoot, and David surprised her by taking her hand in his with Grandfather walking right beside them. Summer didn't pull her hand away. But she was good and confused! David kept acting like he liked her, yet he continued to date Ann. It didn't make sense.

# $S$ixteen

The evening before the race, her grandfather acted very mysterious, but it wasn't until Summer said good-night and started for bed that he called her aside and handed her a package.

Summer sat down on the sofa and allowed Michael to help her unwrap the plaid paper. Everyone laughed when Michael stuck the bow on his forehead and Summer was able to grab the box and open it.

"Oh!" Summer exclaimed, drawing a smile of pleasure from her grandfather.

"Let's have a look," her mother insisted.

Summer was happy to oblige. She pulled the bright emerald-green running outfit from the box and held it up for everyone to see. She then stood up and held the tank top against her. "It's beautiful," she said. "The shorts, too, Grandpa."

"Look at the message," her father suggested.

At Summer's blank expression, her mother added, "The printing on the top of the shirt, honey."

Summer held the top away from her and immediately saw the design, in white, of an impish-looking leprechaun. He seemed to be winking right at her, and she laughed in reaction. "He's darling," she told her grandfather.

"Now look at the back of the shirt," her father instructed.

Summer quickly turned the top around and another gasp of pleasure escaped when she read the words. In small delicate letters near the top of the shirt were the two words, SUMMER'S CHALLENGE, and right below, in bolder, larger print, was the single declaration, EXCELLENCE.

She was too overwhelmed to speak. Tears filled her eyes, and she could only smile and nod her approval.

"What do you think of the color?" her mother asked.

"It's beautiful and very optimistic," Summer said. "I love it."

"The color of Dublin's grass," her grandfather explained. Turning to Summer, he said, "Now remember, it's not important if you win or lose. What counts is the challenge. You've not backed away, girl. You're striving."

"Striving?" her mother repeated.

"Summer," her grandfather said, "explain to your parents what we're talking about."

"Well, Mom and Dad," Summer said, suddenly quite embarrassed, "I'm striving . . . for excellence. Excellence inside me. That's the real challenge . . . not the race."

Her parents seemed to understand, and Summer noticed the special look that passed between them. She smiled again and went to her grandfather. "Thank you, Grandpa," Summer said. She hugged him and whispered in his ear, "For everything, but mostly, for helping me like me."

Her grandfather must have been in a strange mood, for his eyes filled with tears and he had to blow his nose twice before he could turn back to her.

" 'Tis a pleasure girl. A pleasure."

"It's a glorious day, Summer, and time for you to get up." Summer heard her grandfather's voice, booming with cheer. She felt slightly nauseated, but blamed that on her excitement as she bounced out of bed and hurried to look out the window. It was just as the weatherman and her grandfather had predicted, sunny and clear, without a grumpy cloud in sight. Perfect, Summer thought, a perfect day for running! Maybe even winning.

"I don't think I can eat anything," she admitted to her mother at the breakfast table.

"Just nerves, dear. But the race isn't for three more hours and you have to have something in your stomach. Try some toast."

Summer obeyed rather than argue, forcing a slice of the cardboard-tasting bread down. It did help to calm her stomach, but Michael's chatter caused the beginnings of a fierce headache. Summer decided to keep silent about her aches and pains, for she knew that if she complained too much, her mother might decide that she wasn't up to running.

Summer lounged around in her robe until it was finally time to get ready. She took an emergency phone call from Regina and listened with extreme patience while Regina described two outfits.

"Wear the yellow," Summer decided when she could get a word in. "You look great in yellow now that you have a tan."

Summer hung up the phone and went back upstairs. She showered and fixed her hair, and then put on her new running outfit, adding a matching headband. A twirl in front of the mirror made Summer's pounding headache fade, and two aspirins finished the deed.

"Better get started on your warm-ups," her grandfather said, after telling her how pretty she looked.

Everyone — her mother and father, Michael and Grandfather — was waiting for her by the basement steps. Summer laughed at the expectant looks they all wore, and felt very flattered that she had such an enthusiastic audience while she limbered up.

After Grandfather put her through the

paces, everyone piled into her father's station wagon.

By the time they reached the park, Summer's stomach was full of butterflies. She hurried over to the sign-up table and got her number. Regina and Luke found her there, and Regina pinned the tag on Summer's shirt.

"Do you believe this crowd? Mr. Logan says there're over a hundred entered in both the men's and women's divisions. You better start out in front and stay there. Otherwise you might be trampled to death."

Summer looked around and had to agree with Regina. It was quite a crowd. They all looked so professional, too.

"By the way, you look terrific," Regina said. "That outfit is neat."

"Grandpa gave it to me," Summer answered. She saw that her parents were waving and she promptly waved back. Her confidence was dwindling, and Summer didn't know how to stop the fear that was quickly invading her shaking legs. "I just wish they'd get started. Oh, Regina, what if I make a fool of myself?" she whispered so Luke wouldn't overhear. He was busy doing leg bends so she was sure he wasn't paying much attention to their conversation. But she was wrong, for he had heard her and stood up, shaking his head.

"Don't get all nervous. You're good, Summer. Just give it your best shot. And watch that girl over there, the blonde. She's going to be your only real competition. I've seen her in action in other races."

Summer glanced over to where Luke had motioned, and studied the tall girl with interest. She didn't look very formidable, but Summer knew that looks could be deceiving. "Why do you say that?" she asked Luke. I mean, she doesn't look that . . . strong to me."

"She is, though. She took first place in track last year."

"You'll win," Regina said with certainty.

Gregg joined them and he held out his hand to Summer. "Good luck, kid." Before Summer could stop him, he pulled her headband and let go, making a slapping sound against her forehead just like a rubber band.

"Ouch," Summer said as she readjusted her band. She really didn't hurt and knew that was just Gregg's way of being affectionate.

"Has anyone seen David?" Summer glanced around again, squinting against the bright sun as she looked for him.

"There he is, over by that tree," Regina announced. "Don't look, he's staring at you."

Summer of course immediately looked and saw that David was alone. It was now or never. Without giving herself time to waiver, she walked over to him.

"Good luck, David," she said, holding her hand out for a handshake.

"Good luck to you, too," David answered. He took her hand and shook it, but continued to hold on. "I see Gregg came to cheer you on," David continued. "Ann says you two are going steady now. Is that true?"

"Good heavens, no," Summer stuttered. "Why would she say a thing like that?" Summer knew the answer to that. Ann was merely eliminating any competition. She must feel more than a little threatened, after all. Maybe she considered Summer a *real* threat! What a nice thought, Summer decided, gloating.

"Gregg is nothing more than a friend. When I don't have a date, Regina makes him take me."

"Oh, I see," David said.

"What about Ann? I don't see her around," Summer said. "Are you going steady with her?"

"No." David acted embarrassed and his next sentence told Summer why. "She's here all right, but I didn't ask her to cheer me. I don't ask her out, Summer. She calls me and I never know how to say no when she asks me to take her somewhere." His cheeks grew pink and Summer felt sorry for him.

"I think I understand. Ann doesn't know the meaning of no."

"She's a nice girl but I'm not interested in her like I . . ."

"Like what, David?" Summer held her breath and waited.

"I'll tell you after the race. You don't have a date for the picnic, do you?"

"No, I'm here with the family."

"Good," David replied. "I'll meet you right here after the race."

When Summer nodded her agreement, David grabbed her by the shoulders and quickly kissed her, in front of the whole world.

"Is that for luck?" Summer stammered.

"No," David answered. "It's for being you."

In a daze Summer turned and felt like she was floating toward the starting line. Her mind was filled with David's explanation and his kiss, as she nudged into the front line of runners.

All thought of anything but running was placed on hold with the sound of the starting gun. Summer and the girl Luke had pointed out as her biggest competition, were way ahead of the crowd for the first four miles. But from the sounds of panting coming from behind, the challengers were gaining. Summer made her bid then, escalating her pace, feeling free and almost superhuman when victory came into sight. The beckoning ribbon, stretched between two benches, became her focal point. In a final spurt, Summer raced on, a grimace of determination on her face, even as she broke through the ribbon.

Victory was hers! She won by at least a full yard. Her parents and grandfather were all hugging her at once, asking questions and cheering, but Summer was still trying to slow her pulse and get some air, and she could do nothing more than nod her head and cry.

As soon as she received the check for $500.00 and had her picture taken, Summer handed the check over to her father. "Will you take care of this for me, Dad" she asked. "I want to find David."

Before her father could reply, Summer turned and ran over to the spot she and David had agreed on for their meeting place. He was waiting for Summer, leaning against the tree, and he looked genuinely happy.

"I'm sorry that you didn't win," Summer said, "but Grandpa says to tell you that fifth place is nothing to sneeze at. His exact words."

David laughed and hugged her. "I'm so happy that you won, Summer. I'll do better next year."

"Thank you, David," Summer said, trying her best to sound humble.

"It occurred to me that *I'm* the reason you were in this race," David said. "All that work was to impress me, wasn't it?"

Summer was too embarrassed to answer. She shrugged her shoulders instead.

"I acted like a jerk," David said. "I made such a big deal out of your lying, and then I pretended I liked Ann. That's the same as lying, isn't it?"

"Are you saying you're sorry?" Summer asked.

"Did you really like my drawings or were

you lying then, too?" David demanded.

"I liked them."

"Here." David thrust a folder into Summer's hands. She immediately opened it and found a beautiful picture of a runner.

"It's wonderful," Summer said as she studied the picture. "Is it supposed to be me?"

"That's not real tactful, Summer," David said with a chuckle. "Guess it needs a little more work. You're the first nonanimal I've drawn."

"I'll keep this forever," Summer whispered. "Thank you David."

"You're still flushed," David said. "You must have pulled out all the stops. They say you won by a mile."

"Not quite," Summer answered. Impulsively she grabbed his hand and squeezed it. "Thanks for all your help with pacing and everything." It wasn't what she wanted to say. She meant, *I love you, David Marshall.*

"I want to ask you something," David said, a serious expression entering his gaze.

"Yes?"

"I was wondering if . . . uh, if you would like to go steady. You know, just be my girl." David said in a rush. He was looking right into her eyes, and Summer felt like she was going to faint.

"I'd like that," Summer said.

Her answer pleased David considerably, because he grabbed her by the waist and lifted her high into the air. Summer wrapped her arms around his neck and then they both started laughing with delight. This was surely the most wonderful day in her life! Summer closed her eyes tightly and cherished the moment, willing it to last a lifetime. Her eyes slowly opened, and she gazed at her arms. A gasp escaped her. Spots, faint, pink *spots*!

"I don't even care if you lie to me, Summer. You're so much fun to be with," David whispered.

"I'm through with lies," Summer said. She started to laugh and David slowly lowered her to the ground.

"What's so funny?"

"David?" Summer whispered demurely, "Have you ever had the chicken pox?"